Phantom of the Pueblo

Phantom of the Pueblo

JERRY JERMAN

VICTOR BOOKS

A DIVISION OF SCRIPTURE PRESS PUBLICATIONS INC.
USA CANADA ENGLAND

THE JOURNEYS OF JESSIE LAND

The Long Way Home
My Father the Horse Thief
Phantom of the Pueblo
Danger at Outlaw Creek

Cover design by Scott Rattray
Cover illustration by Michael Garland
Copyediting by Afton Rorvik, Liz Duckworth

Library of Congress Cataloging-in-Publication Data

Jerman, Jerry, 1949–
    The phantom of the Pueblo / by Jerry Jerman.
        p.   cm.—(The Journeys of Jessie Land)
    Summary: In June 1935, near Flagstaff, Arizona, Jessie, Leo Little Wolf, and Hazel Womak are entangled in a web of intrigue surrounding an Indian pueblo from which buried Spanish artifacts have mysteriously disappeared.
    ISBN: 1-56476-466-4
    (1. Buried treasure—Fiction. 2. Pueblo Indians—Fiction. 3. Indians of North America—Fiction. 4. Christian life—Fiction. 5. Mystery and detective stories. 6. Arizona—Fiction.) I. Title. II. Series: Jerman, Jerry, 1949– Journeys of Jessie Land.
PZ7.J54Ph   1995
[Fic]—dc20   95-2805
                                                             CIP
                                                             AC

---

1 2 3 4 5 6 7 8 9 10 Printing/Year 99 98 97 96 95

For information write Victor Books,
1825 College Avenue, Wheaton, Illinois 60187.

To my parents

Chapter 1

"That pueblo wall looks like *fresh* mud!" I exclaimed.

Leo shoved past me, edging closer to Hazel to get a gander for himself. The coiled rope tied to his belt flapped against my leg. My anger flared up. My face probably matched his bright, red shirt. God forgive me, but I wanted to grab a handful of his long, unruly, black hair and give that boy a good shake. And since I stood a full head taller than him, I could've done it too.

It was June 1935, the morning of our first day in Arizona, and I didn't much care for the way this trip was starting out. And now our camping trip to explore this old pueblo on Hazel's land had turned mysterious.

The pueblo sat atop a mesa, which was nothing but a kind of flattopped hill. More dry, empty country stretched east and north of us, full of dust and cacti. Hazel had told us all that land made up the Hopi and Navajo Indian reservations. To the south and west of the mesa the land looked lush and green, all covered with pine trees and such. Flagstaff, where Hazel lived, lay miles away in that direction. It was odd, like two different countries stuck plumb together. From where I now stood, I could see

Hazel's airplane below, parked beside a small stream on a level field between the mesa and the forest.

Hazel sniffed the wall in front of us then swiped at it with her fingernails.

"Sure enough is fresh, Jessie Land," she said, "but this ain't plain mud. It has a name—adobe."

I scooted around Leo. After all, *I* had made the discovery. Running my hand over the adobe wall, it felt dry and grainy. But this one part looked darker and felt damp and sticky. Like mud. Frowning, I asked, "But who'd bother to patch up this old wall? You told us yourself this pueblo's probably a hundred years old."

Hazel didn't answer. She wiped her damp face on her shirt sleeve then ran her fingers through her thick, curly, black hair. Although bandanna-red lipstick streaked across her wide mouth, the rest of her looked like a combination of aviator and miner. She wore a dusty, gray flannel shirt and a rope belt cinched her jeans tight around her waist. Her scuffed, high-topped boots looked like those I'd seen in pictures of Charles Lindbergh, the celebrated airplane pilot. You'd never think it to look at her, but Hazel Womack was a woman of considerable means.

I counted her as one of my best friends. She'd helped me find my parents when I first came west. Then she had introduced Daddy to none other than the famed Will Rogers who gave him a job on his Santa Monica ranch. Yesterday, Hazel had flown to California in her shiny red Waco and offered to bring me and Leo to Arizona for a

visit and to camp out on her land where there was a real
Indian pueblo. Mama and Daddy agreed to it right off.

Leo nudged me aside again. Pointing with his stubby
finger, he declared, while chewing a large wad of gum,
"Maybe we oughta jest kick this here wall in and 'vestigate." Before I could stop him, the boy lashed out with
his boot.

"*Leo!*" I cried.

His foot went all the way through the wall, making a
kind of sucking sound. As he yanked his foot out, a thick
piece of adobe clay plopped to the ground at our feet.

"Land o' Goshen," Hazel said. She stooped and grabbed
up a handful of clay, working it in her fingers. Then she
dropped the mud and stood, her face determined.

Leo stepped back, his large, dark eyes shining in his
pudgy, brown face. He wiped his small mouth on his shirt
sleeve and mumbled, "Sorry."

"Nothin' to be sorry for, Leo," Hazel replied, giving
him a hug. "You're a right smart lad. I think we oughta
'vestigate, as you said."

I admit her words riled me a bit. Hazel had taken to
Leo Little Wolf the moment she met him, treating him
like you would a long-lost son. But Hazel had been *my*
special friend. True enough, the boy had no family to call
his own and had been taken in by my folks. The same age
as me, he was a lad to be pitied. Still, I didn't cotton to the
idea of this twelve-year-old "brother" of mine stealing
Hazel away from me.

Hazel retrieved a pick and a shovel from her equipment

box. Pausing in front of the patched wall, she said, "This goes against all the rules. You don't normally tear up anything old. You preserve it. But owing that this pueblo's on my land, I'll just open up the wall a bit so we can 'vestigate easier."

Then she cleared out the patched area with the shovel and widened the opening with the pick.

The job done, she stepped back and wiped the sweat from her face. "That's good," she huffed. "Now let's have a looksee. But careful now. Might be scorpions and such inside. Don't just go landing your hands anywhere."

Leo shrugged. "I ain't afraid of no scorpions or spiders."

That was true enough. I didn't know of many critters he feared. He used to be scared of wolves, but less than a week ago I'd seen him lasso a wolf on Will Rogers' ranch. He saved our very necks that night.

Myself, I didn't much care for scorpions, spiders, or snakes. I hung back and squatted beside the equipment box. In a cracked mirror Hazel used to look at the underside of her plane's engine I caught my reflection. Sure enough, my red hair still looked a mess. Short as a boy's, thanks to my aunt. My brown eyes shined, and I tried to smile. Fact was, I didn't feel much like smiling.

I took a deep breath. Then I stood and stepped through the opening behind Leo and Hazel. Inside, only a little light from above filtered into the dark and dusty-smelling space. The room felt surprisingly cool, and my skin crawled just thinking of the vile things that surely lurked inside.

"Use your feet to feel around," Hazel cautioned. "Keep your hands away from the walls. Might be a black widow or two in here. Their sting'll make you sick as a hound dog."

I plunged my hands deep into my overalls pockets and shuffled around. It didn't take me long to tire of poking about in the small, dark, mud room. Just as I turned to go back outside into the bright warm sunlight—

Thud.

My shoes struck something hard. I stumbled and fell headlong onto the dirt floor.

"Jessie," Hazel called out. "You find something?"

"Just the floor," I cracked.

"Hey, gal," said Leo, "I think you did find somethin'."

He and I felt around until our hands settled on a large box. Hazel knelt beside me.

"Let's scoot it out into the light," she said.

Leo and I pushed the box. Before long, we had it outside in the warm, gleaming sun.

We stood staring at the dusty object like it had come from another planet. Actually, it looked like an old trunk from someone's attic.

"Looks Spanish," Hazel remarked as if to herself.

"Maybe it's a *treasure* chest!" Leo exclaimed, dropping to his knees and fumbling with the lock.

"Hold your horses there, son," Hazel warned, pulling him back.

"Why?" Leo asked.

"Remember the fresh adobe? Someone hid that chest.

Could be the person who's watching us this very moment."

I didn't understand. "What do you mean 'watching us'?"

"Take a gander at those trees," she said, motioning toward the west.

No sooner had we looked that way than a bright light blinded me. I shielded my face and tried to look some more, but I couldn't. It stung my eyes, like looking at the sun.

"Goodness, what's causing that?" I said.

"Likely the reflection off a spyglass or a pair of binoculars," she answered. "Someone's watching every move we make."

Chapter 2

The thought of someone spying on us sent a fierce chill up my back.

"Who could it be?" I asked, hugging myself.

"Don't rightly know," Hazel replied. "But most likely we'll find out."

She then stooped to examine the lock securing the chest. It was a large, rust-covered contraption with a place for a key the size of Hazel's finger. She shook her head.

"Spy or no spy," she began, "I got an itchin' to see what's inside this chest."

"Me too!" Leo sang out as he popped more gum in his mouth.

I was plenty curious myself. I fidgeted as Hazel took hold of the lock and gave it a good, hard yank. The clasp on the rusty hunk of metal broke free, and the lock dropped into the dirt.

"Aha!" cried Hazel.

Leo and I both leaped forward, ready to throw open the old chest and see the contents for ourselves. Owing to how the lid had been stuck closed for lo these many years, it took all three of us to pry it up.

When at last the lid did spring loose, it ripped free from its hinges and flopped a foot away onto the ground.

"What's in there?" Leo asked eagerly. Then he spoke the word that was in my own head. "Treasure?"

Treasure I did hope for. I'll admit it right off. Not that my family needed it. Only a few days ago I'd seen the famed Will Rogers himself plant ten one hundred dollar bills into my father's hand. A reward of sorts for rescuing his favorite horse from horsenappers. With that money we'd be getting our first real home in California. God had richly blessed us. Still, my heart beat faster at the thought of seeing silver and gold inside that chest.

But nothing gleamed under that hot, Arizona sun. What I saw looked like a dried-up animal skin.

"What is it?" I asked Hazel.

"Ah, ain't nothin'," Leo complained, grabbing a fistful of dirt and throwing it in the air. "Ain't no treasure 'tall."

"Well, boy, that depends on what you call treasure," Hazel declared, pulling on a pair of white cotton gloves.

She knelt before the open box and felt the skin with her fingertips. It seemed to be wrapped around something, like a parcel.

"Leo, turn the chest on its side as I pull this skin out," Hazel directed. "I don't want to tear it."

Leo shuffled over and did as he'd been told.

The skin-wrapped object slid out. I saw that the bundle had once been tied with leather strips, but those had rotted and broken away.

When the object lay on the ground, Hazel paused.

"This could be a real find, pardners," she announced. "It sets this old amateur archeologist's heart aflutter just imagining what might be wrapped up in here."

My eyes went to the trees. No trace of the light now. Maybe it hadn't been anything after all. Just the sun's reflection off a bottle or some such thing. I truly hoped no one had been spying on us.

"*Open it!*" Leo cried. I looked at the boy. He hopped from one foot to the other. Chewing his gum furiously, he speculated, "It might be a chunk of gold or somethin' after all."

"Hush," I said, wishing in my secret heart that he spoke the truth. Shame on me for desiring loot!

Hazel carefully pulled apart the skin.

Leo watched her every move, then turned to me. "Aw, shucks," he muttered, disappointed again.

I looked from him to Hazel, whose own face glowed with interest, then back to the ground. There, in our shadow, the animal skin cradled a few rusted objects. Except for a dented metal cup and some coins that looked like pennies, I couldn't identify the "treasure." I noticed black markings on the inside of the skin.

"Why, there's all manner of artifacts here," Hazel said. "Just lookit 'em."

"I'm lookin' but I sure ain't seein' no treasure," Leo announced.

She plucked up what appeared to be a rusted metal shoe with a pointed toe. Truly a funny-looking thing.

"What is that?" I asked her.

"A Spanish stirrup. Sixteenth century, I'd say."

I frowned at the odd piece. "Wouldn't that be awful heavy on a horse?"

"Sure would, Jessie," Hazel answered. "The Spanish explorers who came through here all wore steel armor and a lot of leather and such. Why, I read of a bunch of 'em who drowned when they fell into a river 'cause they were covered head to toe in steel."

She picked up one of the coins. After spitting on it, she rubbed it on her shirt. Then she studied both sides.

"Can't make out none of the writing," she said. "But this looks to me like a Spanish *cuarto*."

Leo grumbled, "Looks like a penny to me."

Nodding, Hazel replied, "It's copper all right. But more like a quarter, you might say."

"A *quarter!*" Leo cried. "That means there ain't no more than a couple of dollars here."

Hazel shook her head. "No, it's more valuable 'cause of its age. But you can't put a price tag on it."

Leo got to his feet, his mouth turned down. He kicked at a mound of adobe mud and twirled his lasso as he walked away.

Turning to me, Hazel remarked, "The real treasure is in what these things tell us about the past. This chest might date back to Coronado."

"Coronado? You mean the explorer who searched for the gold cities?"

"Yep," she said with a smile. "The Seven Cities of

Cibola. Only there wasn't any Cibola. Or seven cities either. The Indians who lived back then just told the explorers that so they'd leave 'em alone. And Coronado and the others believed the Indians' stories. Their lust for gold killed a good many men."

I watched Leo expertly lasso a wooden beam poking up from the rubble of a collapsed room.

Hazel's voice got low. "If word gets out that we've found this chest, it could get a little dangerous around here. There're still a few treasure-hungry Coronados running around. Yep. Could get even more than a little dangerous."

Chapter 3

That word *dangerous* whizzed past my head like a bullet. I wanted to ask her what she meant, but all of a sudden I heard a ferocious roar at the base of the mesa.

We got up to take a look below. A car exploded across the rocky, forlorn Arizona landscape, coming at us like a fierce thunderstorm.

Hazel's eyes stayed on the vehicle. "Uh-oh," she muttered. "That danged Cal Maddox."

"Who?" I asked.

"Cal Maddox. He's a rancher. Got a big spread next to my land just to the south. He—"

The motor's rumble interrupted her. Even Leo, who'd been twirling his lasso, threw down his rope to cover his ears with his hands.

Hazel, Leo, and I stayed at the edge of the mesa, though I didn't care a whit for the noise of that infernal machine.

As the roaring black car splashed through the stream below and skidded to a stop, it threw a cloud of dust into the air that came swirling up past the top of the mesa. Hazel glanced at us.

"You kids move back," she declared. "This man's trouble."

But I had to see for myself. Leo and I stuck with her at the mesa's edge.

"What ya reckon this galoot wants?" Leo asked, right behind me.

"I guess we'll find out," I told him.

The driver's door burst open. A large man shot out of the car, slamming the door behind him. He stood tall and threatening. His clothing seemed to reflect the sun and it hurt my eyes to look at him. I thought of the light we'd seen coming from the trees.

"Thunderation, Hazel Womack, where is she?" the man boomed, almost seeming to shake the ground. *"I know she headed this way!"*

Instead of waiting for an answer, the man charged up a path to the top of the mesa. He got there in no time.

He stood at the edge of the mesa like he wanted us to inspect him. So I did.

I noticed his boots first. Highly polished reddish-brown, with silver tips. The man had silver tips on his collar to match the ones on his boots. He wore a string tie with a large, silver clasp. When he yanked off his white cowboy hat and mopped his forehead with his shirtsleeve, I saw a huge, silver ring on his finger. This man liked his silver, that much was clear. Even his shaggy hair was silver. A lock of it hung down over his lined forehead. He glared at Hazel.

Hazel strode right up to him. Hands on her hips, she

looked him in the eye and declared, "You're not welcome on my land. Turn that noisy heap around and clear out."

Cal Maddox stood his ground.

"Not without Areana I won't," he roared. "You can't tell me she's not around here somewhere."

"Fact is, I can do just that," Hazel replied. "I ain't seen her 'tall."

They railed on at each other for a time. The man didn't even seem to notice children present. Usually, a child on the scene settles folks down. I've seen it plenty of times.

Maddox's red face loomed inches from Hazel's. He continued to rave about someone named Areana.

Finally, I cleared my throat and said, "Hazel, it's almost noon. You want me to start fixing lunch?"

Maddox turned his gaze on me. He'd never seen me before, but that didn't take the fire out of his eyes. He did stop his ranting at Hazel. I'll grant him that.

"What have we here?" he asked. "Who is this upstart? And that one over there?" He meant Leo.

A fire all my own flared up in me at the word *upstart*. I told him, "If it's any business of yours, we're friends of Hazel. Visiting from California."

He ignored my anger and said, "And where's Henry?" Henry was Hazel's brother.

"You're about the nosiest ol' buzzard I have ever met," Hazel replied.

Her answer didn't suit him. He insisted, "Well, where is he? Has he taken sick?"

Hazel's thick, black eyebrows darted up. "You worried

about Henry now? I thought it was just Areana. If you hafta know, Henry's off to Nevada, meeting someone who wants to buy some property of ours. Now if you're through asking pesky questions, Cal Maddox, I'd 'preciate your getting outta here."

But Maddox seemed set on staying. He took another gander at me and then looked toward the pueblo. He spied something and I knew what it was.

The chest.

"What's that there?" he asked, frowning.

He took three long strides toward the chest and stopped. I stood in his way.

"Step aside, child," he declared.

I knew what the Bible said about respecting your elders, but I confess that I stood my ground.

"I said 'step aside,' " he repeated, louder.

"You'll find folks a lot more sociable if you don't order them about so," I told him.

He looked at me like he couldn't believe what he'd just heard. He asked Hazel, "What's this upstart's name?"

"Jessie Land," I piped up.

To me he said, "I don't recollect asking you."

"I'm fully able to give my own name," I said.

I guess he grew tired of fooling with me because he just started around me in the direction of the chest.

"*Whoa* there, Maddox!" Hazel cried out. "I never invited you over here. You clear off my land or you'll be dealing with the law."

Maddox halted. He'd heard Hazel all right, but his eyes

focused on the chest. I spied the man's jaw muscles clench. I could tell it ate at him. Not knowing what that box contained.

"You heard me," Hazel said. "We ain't seen Areana and that's that. Now clear out."

Suddenly, Maddox's voice erupted like a volcano. "You mark my words, woman. If you're lying to me, you'll wish it was that blasted *phantom* and not me who gets his clutches on you!"

Suddenly a lasso curled in the air above us and dropped expertly over Cal Maddox's shoulders.

Leo!

"Thunderation!" Cal Maddox cried.

The rancher yanked himself free, then fired at us a look that could have burned rocks. He shook with rage as he tore down the mesa, stomped back toward his car, and climbed in. The car bolted in reverse, the engine thundering. Goodness, the man sure could bluster.

But I sensed something more than bluster to this man. And I admit, it frightened me no little bit.

We watched the car until it became a speck. All the while his words repeated in my mind. Finally, I looked at Hazel and asked, "What was it he made mention of—a *phantom?*"

Chapter 4

I've never been given to superstition and such, so I just stood there waiting for Hazel to explain. I glanced at Leo. He'd stopped chomping his gum. His lasso lay limp on the ground.

"Phantom?" he whispered, as if afraid to speak the word out loud. "You mean like a ghost?"

Hazel began, "Couple months ago some archeologists ol' Maddox hired were digging near here on the Hopi reservation. They started hearing eerie sounds at night. Kinda like flute music, they said.

"They figured it was just the Hopis," she continued. "Then stranger things happened. One day while they worked, someone piled up some of their tents and burned 'em. And every morning they'd come back to the dig and find the dirt shoveled back in, covering up what they'd uncovered the day before. They tried posting a guard. But the next day the guard would always quit, claiming to have seen a mysterious figure—the phantom, he came to be called. They also claimed to've heard groaning, animal-like sounds. And seen some strange tracks. Then they dug up a—"

Hazel's eyes widened. She looked back at the old chest. Her mouth dropped open, but she said nothing.

"What's the matter?" I asked. "What'd they dig up?"

"A *chest!*" she exclaimed. "They dug up a Spanish chest they thought might've dated back to the 1500s."

"You mean *this* one?" I said pointing at our discovery.

"Might possibly be, child," she said.

"But how'd it get here?" Leo wanted to know.

Hazel shook her head. "Don't rightly know. They said the chest disappeared one night. That proved to be the last straw for those fellas. They packed up and left for good. A few poor folks they'd hired to help on the dig babbled about the phantom taking the chest. Maddox—he was fit to be tied when those archeologists took off."

"But if the phantom, or whoever it was, took the chest, why would he hide it here on your land?" I asked.

"Don't know," she admitted. "But I reckon we'll figure it out."

Leo hadn't moved to pick up his rope. He still stared straight ahead with that big wad of gum bulging in his cheek. I knew all this phantom talk scared him.

Spooks and such didn't have much effect on me. I knew they were purely imaginings. I believed in God as ruler of all things. If spooks and phantoms haunted His kingdom, you could've looked it up in the Bible, like you could angels.

"Hey, listen up, cowboys and cowgirls," Hazel sang out, looking at Leo. "We're here to explore, not tell ghost stories. So let's get busy."

I tried to put the mysterious phantom out of my mind. I wanted to forget about being spied on too, but somehow those two things still stuck in my head.

"The word *pueblo*'s Spanish for village or town," Hazel explained, as we walked back to the pueblo. The ruins looked like a bunch of square, flat-roofed buildings shoved together, growing out of the rocky landscape.

Hazel told us, "Every one of those rectangular boxes is a room. But to the Indians who lived here, a room was their whole house. As the population grew, they just built on more houses. Some right next to each other. Some on top of each other. Some pueblos went up five stories or more."

I stood in front of the pueblo amazed that the whole thing had been made of dirt. Adobe clay, Hazel called it, but dirt just the same. I'd seen a sod house once in Oklahoma, built by a farmer who couldn't afford wood, but I'd never heard of building a whole town of earth.

"They look like boxes all stacked up," I told her.

"Yep. And they're all situated around a plaza."

She led us into a large, open area in the midst of the adobe box-houses.

"This's where most everything happened," Hazel pointed out. "Folks slept in the houses. They planted and harvested out in the fields. But festivals and ceremonies and dances and such all happened here in the plaza."

Leo raced past us and headed for an old stick ladder leaning against a wall.

"Careful, son," Hazel commanded. "Most of those ladders are rotten. And stay off the roofs. The ones that haven't caved in yet will if you sneeze hard enough."

Leo ignored her warning and stepped up on the ladder. His foot crunched right through the bottom rung. He grabbed hold of the next rung. It came apart in his hand.

"Shucks," he muttered in disgust as he walked away, kicking at stones in the plaza.

I looked about the pueblo, wondering about the inhabitants. "What did these folks grow?" I asked Hazel.

"Corn mostly," she replied. "Most everything they ate had corn in it. They ground corn with milling stones in these trough-like contraptions."

I tried to picture what it must have been like living in a pueblo. I thought about grinding up corn with stones and thought of all the fine grains of sand and rock folks'd be eating. It put me in mind of living back in Kansas with my aunt during those vile dust storms. All night long I'd sleep with a damp towel over my face, but in the morning I'd still be spitting dust.

Then I noticed something odd.

"Hazel, I don't see any doors on the downstairs rooms, only on the upper ones."

She patted me on the back.

"Good observation, Jessie," she said. "Before the 1880s, the Indians stored food in some of the ground floor rooms. Since they were scared other tribes would raid them and steal the food, they built these rooms without doors. They'd enter through hatchways in the roof with ladders going down. The upper rooms had doors, and they climbed ladders to get up there. If they saw enemies a-comin', they'd just haul up the ladders and be safe. Simple as that."

I heard a distant sound. Leo? Where'd he go off to?

Suddenly I remembered the reflection and the spy. Even with Hazel next to me, I felt uneasy. Like someone might still be watching us.

Nonsense, Jessie Land, I told myself. *Get those fool notions out of your head. You're safe here.*

Just then Leo appeared in an opening between two adobe rooms. He waved at us to come. Then, pointing behind him, he shouted, "Hey, someone's comin'!"

Chapter 5

I raced past Leo to get a gander at the new arrival.

She had climbed up the trail and now stood on the edge of the mesa. Slapping a pair of riding gloves against her dusty, tan trousers, she gazed at us with dark, sad eyes.

Right off, I considered her one of the prettiest young women I'd ever seen. She wore a white blouse and dark-brown riding boots. Around her neck dangled a simple gold cross. Her long, black hair, parted in the middle, hung down straight and loose.

As I walked over to greet her, I nearly gasped at her true loveliness. The smooth skin on her oval face looked like a polished stone. Her bright, dark eyes studied me. A sweet-smelling fragrance came from her.

She smiled slightly and nodded, dropping her eyes the way a shy person will.

I wiped my hand on my overalls, then stuck it out to her. "I'm Jessie Land," I said.

She slid her thin, cool hand in mine. "Areana Maddox," she said, almost whispering.

Cal Maddox's daughter! Could this lovely creature belong to that feisty man?

I told her, "We just had a visit from your—"

"Father," she whispered, looking away again as she spoke the word. "I am not surprised."

"He was so angry ab—"

"He's forever angry about something," she said, her gaze drifting toward the pueblo.

Areana looked back to me and said, "I didn't know Hazel had children."

"She doesn't," I replied. "Me and Leo are just visiting. We live in California. That's where my—"

"Your parents are?" she said. I noticed then that she had a habit of completing my sentences for me. In another person, it would've been plain irritating, but I had already grown fond of this pretty, soft-spoken young woman. "But the boy—Leo, is it? He doesn't really look like you. He's your brother?"

I glanced back at Leo. Hazel came up beside him and put her arm around his shoulders. She took a gander at Areana and then waved. Areana waved back.

Shaking my head, I told her, "No. My parents took—"

"Took him in?" She nodded, more it seemed to herself than to me. "It's these awful times we're in. So many people without homes. So many families broken up."

I felt strangely drawn to this quiet beauty, and I wanted her to stay and talk, so I asked, "How long have you lived h—?"

"*Here?* In Arizona?" she interrupted. "I was born here,

on my father's ranch."

She gazed at me, then reached out with her delicate hand to touch my hair.

"Do you normally wear your hair in this fashion?" Areana asked.

She meant cropped short like a boy's. I could almost smile about it now. I shook my head. "My aunt in Kansas cut it. I was staying with her a while back. She didn't seem to like—"

"Bothering with it?" she said. "A pity. You have such beautiful red hair. Like copper. I like your eyes too. A nice, rich brown."

"Thanks," I said. I felt my face flush, getting so many compliments all at once.

She took a few steps toward Hazel and called out, "My car got stuck. Could you give me a hand with it? It was fortunate I was towing Midnight or I'd never have gotten this far."

"What's Midnight?" I asked.

"My mare."

Hazel's raspy voice shot back, "Funny you should come out this way without knowing anyone was about."

"A lucky guess," Areana replied quickly.

I watched as Hazel pulled Leo closer and asked in her loud voice, "How 'bout it, pardner? Shall we give this damsel a hand?"

Leo smiled and nodded. "Can I ride the horse?"

I turned quickly away. *Of course he'd get to ride the horse,* I thought. *Of course he would.*

* * *

It was quite a trek to Areana's broken-down car.

Naturally, when we climbed down the mesa, Leo got his chance to ride Midnight, Areana's spirited black mare. Hazel hiked along beside him.

Areana started to join them, but I took her arm and we walked together. I hung back so we kept our distance from the other two.

"Don't you care about riding Midnight?" she asked.

"I've done my share of riding," I replied, casting a glance ahead to see Hazel and Leo whooping it up. Every time Leo let out a holler or a *"yee-hi!,"* it stabbed my heart—the pangs of jealousy.

As Areana and I made our way across the stony ground, I felt her eyes on me.

"There is a problem between you and the boy?" she said softly. The whisper of her words tickled my spine, giving me a chill.

"Leo and me?" I asked, trying to look surprised. "We're good friends."

It felt like a lie when I said it, but I just couldn't explain it to a near stranger. I was having plenty of trouble explaining it to myself. I admit my thoughts stuck on Leo and how Hazel had taken such a shine to him. I told myself, *Jessie Land, stop being a fool. You know Leo's your true friend. Hazel too.*

Areana grasped my arm tight and seemed to be trying to hold me back. I looked at her and knew she wanted me

to talk, to explain how I felt about Leo. I just couldn't. I
pulled myself loose and ran toward her stranded vehicle.

Since Leo rode Midnight all over, just enjoying himself,
I reached the car first, a green convertible with spoked
wheels. A horse trailer was hooked up behind it.

While I waited for the others, I climbed into the backseat. Beside me in the seat I noticed two paintings. Before I had a chance to look at them, though, Hazel and
Leo came along.

Areana soon tramped up. She mumbled something to
Hazel. Then she climbed in the driver's seat and tried
starting the car. It just made a ru-ru-ru-ru-ru sound. Hazel looked under the hood.

"Hey, gal, you want to ride?" Leo called to me.

Areana turned around in the front seat and looked at
me. Like she expected me to say or do something to
show there was "a problem" between me and Leo.

To prove her wrong, I climbed out of the car and answered, "Sure, Leo."

He got down and I pulled myself up into the saddle. It
creaked as I adjusted myself. I felt the horse's strength
beneath me. It seemed like she could bolt in an instant
and just run forever.

"Keep a tight rein on 'er," Leo advised. "She's powerful."

I trotted her out to an outcropping of rock near where
the forest began. She gave me no trouble, but only because I did what Leo told me. If I'd let loose of the reins,
no telling where we'd end up.

After a while, I rode her back to the car. No sooner had
I climbed down than Leo swung back in the saddle.

Hazel looked up from the engine and sang out, "Stay
clear of that forest, Leo. There's an abandoned mine in
there. The ground's bound to be unstable."

I climbed into the backseat again next to the paintings.
I admit my curiosity got the better of me. With Areana
sitting there looking at me, I pulled up one of the paintings.

When I saw it, I just stared. I couldn't believe it. A picture of a woman. The face of smooth, polished stone, the
sad eyes, the long, dark hair. *Areana!* Yet the fine wrin-
kles around the eyes and mouth and the faint gray in the
hair did not belong to the young woman in the front seat.
In the lower right-hand corner I spied the name printed in
a childlike scrawl: *Areana.*

"You painted this!" I exclaimed.

Nodding shyly, she whispered, "I was taking them to a
gallery in Flagstaff when my car broke down."

I studied the rich colors in the painting. The woman
wore a bright-red dress. A green fan lay in her lap. In one
hand, she held a bunch of blue straw flowers. In the
other, she squeezed a shiny, silver necklace.

Areana asked, "Do you like it?"

"Oh, yes," I said, looking at her. "It's wonderful. But
who is it? It looks—"

"Like me? Yes." Her mouth trembled slightly as she
spoke the words: "It's my mother."

I said, "I'd like to meet her." I meant it too.

"She died long ago. I painted it from a photograph. And I spent a lot of time gazing into the mirror too, since everyone says I so resemble her."

Areana's eyes looked so sad at that moment that I had to look away. I examined the second painting, a smaller one. It pictured a young man's face with dark, angry eyes and a hard mouth. He looked like he'd never smiled. Part of his unruly, jet-black hair fell over his eyes. He wore a brown, ruffled shirt. With the dark background, it seemed to me like a portrait of a man hiding in a cave.

I looked at Areana. "Who—"

Hazel's voice barked from the front of the car. "OK, Areana. Give it a try now."

Areana started to turn away, but I grabbed her arm and said, "I'd like to know—"

"Who he is?" she whispered. "My brother."

I wanted to ask more, but she swung away and tried the car's engine. It started right up.

Hazel came from the front of the car, wiping her hands on a dirty bandanna and frowning.

"Mighty strange," she remarked, her voice raspy. "Nothing wrong with the engine. A couple of wires pulled loose is all. Almost like they—"

"Like they worked themselves loose?" Areana said. "Yes. It's happened before with this car."

Hazel's attention strayed to Leo and Midnight. She set off in that direction. What was it about that boy that attracted her so?

With nary a word, Areana hopped out of the car, reached

in back, fetched the paintings, and hustled them into the horse trailer. When she reappeared, she yelled to Leo and Hazel, *"Time to go back!"*

Peculiar is the name I give to such behavior.

* * *

When Areana dropped us off at the base of the mesa, the sun already sat on the horizon. Red plumes shot out across a purple sky so beautiful that I hardly noticed her pull away in her green car. Leo took off up the mesa, lasso in hand, leaving me alone with Hazel for about the first time that day.

"Did you know Areana paints pictures?" I asked.

"Sure 'nough?" Hazel said, watching Leo climb and not paying me any mind at all.

"You could've seen them for yourself," I said, irritated. "Two of them were in the back seat of her car. One of her mother and the other of her brother."

My words seemed to catch her off guard. "Her *brother?*" she asked, frowning at me.

"Yes. Black hair, dark eyes, very serious looking."

"Well, that's just impossible," she announced.

"Why?"

"Areana don't have a brother. Or sister neither. Her mama died birthin' her. Ol' Cal Maddox hasn't been married since."

I felt a chill at the back of my neck. This was just plain odd. Before I could ask Hazel more, Leo's voice rang out from above, *"Hazel! Jessie! Git on up here quick!"*

We hightailed it up the mesa and into the ruins to join him.

"What's the matter?" I asked, out of breath.

"Lookit," he said, his eyes wide, his finger pointing at the wall we'd broken open earlier that day.

"Land o' Goshen!" Hazel declared, coming up behind me.

We all stood and stared. The wall had been covered over again with fresh adobe. The chest was gone, but a track in the dust told us it had been dragged back inside. Just where we'd first discovered it.

Chapter 6

I shivered in my bedroll. The night air chilled me true enough, but other things kept me awake. Like the mystery of Areana and her family. And the strange repair of the pueblo wall. And the reflection off that spyglass. I shut my eyes and tried to sleep. But too much had happened.

Hazel's earlier warning about it getting "mighty dangerous" if anyone found out about the Spanish chest came back to me. I imagined all sorts of things in the dark. Villains creeping up while we slept. Treasure-hungry folks threatening us if we didn't turn over what we'd found. And in my imaginings came the face of that Cal Maddox fellow. I saw again the way he'd exploded onto the scene with that noisy car and his threats to Hazel.

Then I remembered the talk about a phantom.

It all swirled in my brain, keeping me wide awake. I smelled the faint trace of wood smoke and glanced at the dying embers of the campfire. Beside it Hazel snored like a clogged automobile horn. I heard Leo's heavy breathing, telling me he was deep in sleep.

A night hawk or some such bird cried out, but it didn't

cause me any alarm. I'd heard them plenty back in Oklahoma and Kansas. Even the whistling wind or the presence of the huge old pueblo just a few feet away didn't spook me.

Only the stuff in my head troubled me.

I felt tired from the long day. So much had happened since we left home in Santa Monica that morning. I longed for a deep, sound sleep. *Dear Lord,* I prayed, *help me . . .*

Through the wind came a faint whistling sound.

I sat up in a flash.

What was *that?* My heart racing, I listened close. Had the sound been real? Or merely the wind or my imagination.

When it didn't come again, I resettled myself in my bedroll. *Jessie Land, you've gone and spooked yourself good. Now finish your prayers and go to sleep.*

I sighed and shut my eyes.

A clear, musical sound drifted past me. It sounded too melodic to be just the wind. The soft tune continued a while. Then stopped.

I yanked the blanket over my head.

"Oh my goodness, oh my goodness," I said over and over again.

My heart beat so loudly I just knew it would wake Hazel and Leo. Under the covers I listened. All I could hear, though, was Hazel's snores.

Then as I pulled the blanket off my head, I heard it again. Very clearly. A melody. Made by some kind of musical instrument.

"I'm not afraid," I whispered to myself. "I'm in God's hands." I shoved the blanket off and, shivering, pulled on my shoes. I knew I'd never sleep until I knew the reason for that sound. I'd best go 'vestigate, as Leo would say.

I glanced over at him. He lay sleeping on one side of the fire, with Hazel on the other.

"Leo," I whispered. "Hazel."

They didn't stir. Instead, Hazel's car horn snoring grew louder and Leo sighed, deep in sleep.

What if I woke them and the sound just turned out to be the wind whistling though the nearby pueblo or some such thing? How Leo'd howl about that. He and Hazel would have themselves a grand time laughing at me.

Jessie Land, the fool child who hears strange sounds in the dark.

No. I decided to go it alone. Hopping to my feet, I set out into the pueblo.

The tune began anew. I stopped and listened. I realized then that it sounded something like a penny whistle. I'd had one myself, back in Kansas when I lived with my aunt and her family. It disappeared and I figured my cousin, Walter, stole it.

The night air made me shiver. I hugged my chest as I picked my way over the rocky ground. In the moonlight the pueblo seemed eerie and mysterious. I reckoned it held a secret in every one of its shadows.

The faint melody continued. The music sounded pretty and sad at the same time. And a mite scary. I admit that.

My heart pounded and I stood still in the darkness.

Finally, I told myself, *Get going. Being scared of flute music is pure childishness. You've been in lots worse scrapes than this. Why, you could hardly call this a scrape at all.*

I took a deep breath, then went on.

Running my hand along the cool, rough adobe wall, I leaned in the direction of the flute music. I could hear it clearer now.

It came from the far side of the pueblo.

I stepped over the rubble of crumbled adobe and splintered beams, balancing myself with one hand on a wall. This way, I edged around to the open space called the plaza.

Here, Hazel had told us, the Indians had held their ceremonies and religious events. It seemed a likely place to find a phantom flute player.

When I thought the word, I stopped short. *Phantom.* What had Hazel said about the phantom who tormented those archeologists? He'd burned their tents and stolen their findings. He'd spooked them until they all ran off.

But there's no such thing as phantoms, I told myself. God Himself rules the spirit world. This phantom talk is pure foolishness.

Jessie Land, stop your nonsense and find the culprit blowing that flute. Now!

I braced myself and, with a deep breath and a silent prayer, walked on.

The sound seemed to be drifting out from a mound of rubble across the plaza. I saw no one. Crouching, I crept forward into the open space. Much as I tried not to, I made plenty of racket. My feet kept kicking stones and stray chunks of wood. Anyone out there got plenty of warning I was coming.

Finally, I reached the rubble. The flute music stopped.

I squatted, pressed my hands on the ground, and gasped for air. And courage. Then, springing up, I raced around the rubble pile, hoping to surprise the culprit.

On the other side of the mound, I halted. No one! Thinking the mysterious musician might have ducked into one of the houses nearby, I darted forward. As I ran, I stumbled and pitched headlong.

"Ahhh!" I cried out as I fell.

My knees and hands struck the ground first, hard, and I skidded into the dirt. The dry taste of dust puffed up into my mouth and I coughed. Then I caught a movement out of the corner of my eye.

I shot to my feet and bolted after the dark shape. The flute player? I didn't know, but I had to find out.

Every step I took crashed in my ears. How could this flute player move around without making any noise? I thought I caught a movement ahead, near a ladder propped against the side of a house. I dashed that way, but when I reached the ladder I saw nothing at all.

Then the tune started up again.

It came from the roof!

As I grabbed for the ladder, Hazel's words came back to me. "Stay off the ladders and the roofs," she'd said. I paused a moment thinking over her warning. But this chase had become like a game of hide and seek to me. I felt *so* close! I *wanted* to find that flute player!

I made my way up the rickety ladder, taking an extra big step where one of the rungs was broken. As I climbed, the music grew louder. I had that phantom now, I just knew I did. One old ladder and one crumbling building weren't nearly enough to deter Jessie Land.

When I reached the top, I stopped. The moon lit up the whole rooftop. No one! The flute player had disappeared.

I stepped lightly onto the roof. I wouldn't make the mistake of going out in the middle where Hazel said it was most likely to cave in.

I inched along the edge of the roof. Then a clunk behind me startled me. As I twisted to look back, I felt my foot slip.

The roof started crumbling beneath me! My body pitched forward. I tried to scream, but it never came out.

For a second only the rush of wind held me up.

Then I started to fall.

At once an arm swept around me and tugged me back. I struggled to reach around and cling to whoever had rescued me. My hands clutched a bare arm and a scrap of soft wool. Arms gathered me in and my chest heaved as I gulped for air.

A pleasant fragrance came from my rescuer. I looked up into Areana's dark eyes. A faint smile clung to her lips.

"You must be careful, Jessie," she said softly. "These rooftops are very fragile."

"But how'd you get up here?" I gasped. "Are you the—"

"The phantom?" she interrupted, knowing my thoughts. Her soft laugh drifted in the air like the flute music. Like the scent of her perfume. "You must go down at once. Here, let me help you."

"But—"

"Time for questions when we get down," she said.

She led me back to the ladder and helped me over the edge of the roof. I started down, then stopped.

"You're coming too, aren't you?" I asked.

Smiling, she seemed to nod. I went down a few steps, stopped, and looked up. I didn't see her. So I climbed back up the ladder.

As I peered over the roof, I felt a chill on the back of my neck. No sign of Areana. She had disappeared!

I clung to the ladder. What was happening? I hadn't imagined nearly falling from the roof or Areana saving me. Those things had been real.

The night air bit through my clothes. The moonlight lit the landscape with a cool glow. I could see to the edge of the mesa. The campfire where Hazel and Leo slept glowed. It all looked so peaceful, so ordinary.

But I didn't feel at peace. And this was no ordinary place. Something strange was going on here. Something very strange.

Chapter 7

By the time I crawled back into my bedroll, I felt so tired nothing could keep me awake. Not even the strange rustling I heard near the edge of the mesa where Hazel had stored our food and supplies. No eerie shadows, no odd flute music, not even Areana's mysterious appearance would keep me from a deep, sound sleep.

I woke at Hazel's rasping cry.

"Who did this?"

I blinked at the morning sun, my head still full of a dream I'd been having of being lost in a dark forest.

When I sat up, my legs felt like lead. Like I really had been running all night.

Leo stuck his face in mine. He said, "Gal, did you git into our grub last night?"

Most times I wake up friendly enough, but not when I'm wrongly accused of misdeeds.

"Go away, Leo," I snapped.

Hazel ambled up behind him. She frowned at the forest spread out below the mesa.

"Seems someone sneaked into our camp last night and stole our food," she barked.

"Who?" Leo and I sang out at the same time.

"Don't rightly know," she admitted. "I do know one thing. I'm gonna have to fly to Flagstaff for more food if we aim to stay out here." She hefted a worn canvas bag. "All we got to eat now are a handful of dry biscuits and a few wormy apples."

Wiping the sleep from my eyes, I dug an orange from my pocket.

"I've got this," I offered. "I was saving it for later."

"Best save it, child," Hazel said. "You might get hungry later."

I climbed to my feet and stared at the pueblo. Strange. I half expected it to be changed somehow after my search for the flute player. *And Areana!* Could *she* have stolen our food? I knew I should tell Hazel about seeing Areana in the pueblo. But at that moment, I couldn't bring myself to do it.

While Hazel warmed the biscuits by the fire and sliced the apples, I put up my bedroll. Leo stuffed a cold biscuit into his mouth and practiced some rope tricks.

As I ate, I kept thinking about the events of last night. I'd chased *something.* No, some*one.* Could the phantom be real? Not a ghost but a flesh and blood person trying to spook us. And could it be Areana? Why would she carry on in such a way? None of it made sense. Areana didn't. Nor her father. Yet there must be an answer, some explanation for all of this.

When I took my last bite, Hazel said, "You kids can just leave your things here. We'll fly to Flagstaff and be back in a couple of hours."

Leo stopped twirling his rope and groaned.

"What's wrong?" Hazel said.

"Do we hafta go?" he whined.

I gazed at him. His face looked whitewashed, it was so pale. Just like it had yesterday flying over California and Arizona. No doubt about it. Leo, or leastwise his stomach, didn't take much to airplane rides.

"An airplane jest can't compare with a horse," he bluffed. "If we was ridin' horseback to Flagstaff, then I'd be itchin' to go."

"So what do you have in mind?" Hazel asked him.

"Jessie and me could jest wait here," he suggested. "Do some explorin' and such."

"I don't think that's such a good idea with food thieves about," Hazel said.

"The food thief's already got the food," he argued. "Besides, we'd be careful, wouldn't we, gal?"

They turned to me. For once I didn't really have an opinion. I shrugged and said, "We'll be OK here."

Hazel squinted at us, seeming to size us up. Then she nodded. "Well, I reckon if you two can catch horse thieves, you'll be all right on your own for a couple of hours." She was speaking about how we'd caught some horsenappers in California. A reporter fellow wrote it all up in the local newspaper. "Well, then, I'll head out. How 'bout you giving me a hand turning the Waco around?"

I wiped my fingers on my overalls and followed Hazel and Leo down the mesa. With Hazel about to leave and all, I decided I'd best tell her the events of last night.

At the base of the mesa, I said, "Someone played a flute in the pueblo last night."

"The wind," she replied, leading us through the shallow stream. "Sounds kinda flute-like sometimes, specially at night."

"But I got up and chased after it. I saw someone on—" I stopped short. I didn't want to confess to being on that roof. I added, "Not just someone—Areana."

"Goodness, child, what a dream you had!" she exclaimed, patting my cheek with her rough fingers.

"But it *wasn't* a dream," I insisted. "It—"

"Help me swing the tail around," she said, ignoring my words. "I'll get the engine started and be on my way."

I gave up. I admit it sounded like a dream. But I also knew it *hadn't* been one.

Leo and I hefted the plane's tail and walked it around in a half circle so the nose now faced the long stretch of field. As Hazel climbed into the cockpit, I thought I saw something in the line of trees off to our right.

"Did you see that?" I asked Leo, pointing.

"See what?" he replied.

"Over there, in the trees. I thought I saw something move. Something dark."

He glanced at the trees. "Gal, you've been hearin' too many spook tales and havin' too many dreams. I don't see nothin' but trees."

I squinted at the forest. Only trees. Maybe he was right. Probably just my imagination playing tricks on me.

When I looked back at the plane, I caught Hazel whis-

pering something to Leo. So now they had secrets, those
two. I began to think maybe Hazel's leaving us for a time
was a good thing.

"OK, cowboys and cowgirls, listen up," Hazel barked at
us. "This trip'll take me two, maybe three hours. I might
stop and talk to someone at the museum. About that
chest. You two be careful. Stick together. If you explore
the pueblo, stay off the ladders and roofs. Hear me?"

We both nodded.

With that, she pulled on her goggles and started the
plane's engine. It fired up right away. I yelled for her to
be careful and watched as the Waco taxied down the strip
of level ground, picking up speed as it went.

I said a silent prayer for her safety just as the plane
jerked up and began its climb. It looked like a red bird
gliding through the clear, blue sky.

Leo and I scampered back up the trail to the top of the
mesa. There, I stood watching Hazel's plane as it swung
in a wide arc to the south, toward Flagstaff.

Leo tugged at my arm.

"Come on, gal, let's get to explorin'," he urged.

"Hold your horses, Leo," I told him. "I want to watch
Hazel till she's out of sight."

Looking out over the landscape, I wished Mama and
Daddy could've seen this peaceful place. All God's handi-
work. Lovely as it could be. The rocky mesa rising from
the plain below. The forest off to the south over which
Hazel's plane now flew. The cloudless, blue sky hanging
over it all. To some folks it'd seem empty, sure enough.

Still, it was one of the prettiest places I'd ever seen.

At that moment I heard something odd. A sputter. The sound of a machine not working properly. Hazel's plane!

I gasped.

"What—" Leo began but didn't finish.

The red Waco wobbled in the sky.

"No, no!" I cried. "Dear God. *Hazel!"*

But my cry wouldn't help her. The plane pitched down and made an awful whining sound as it dropped. Leo and I stood, horrified, and watched Hazel's tiny, red airplane disappear into the dark forest.

Chapter 8

Hot tears sprang to my eyes. My breath came in gasps. I stared unbelieving at the empty sky. *This can't be happening. Dear God in heaven, this just can't be!* Then a thin snake of black smoke curled up.

I grabbed Leo and held on to him. For a time we kept standing there, unmoving, not believing what we'd just seen.

Then my disbelief turned into something else.

"We've gotta get over there, Leo!" I gasped. "Hazel might be hurt."

Hurt? The word sounded ridiculous in my ears, but I couldn't say out loud what I really feared. That Hazel might be dead.

"You're right, g-g-gal," he stuttered. "Let's git goin'." Worry clouded his face. I knew he wouldn't speak our worst fear.

I took one last look at the smoke rising from the forest, then rushed back to camp. I grabbed a canteen and the first-aid kit Hazel had brought with us. We had no food save for the orange in my overall pocket.

"I'll git matches, gal," Leo suggested. "We might need

to make a fire."

I looked at my friend, relieved. Dear Leo! The boy had managed to keep his wits about him. We needed our wits about us now more than ever. The place where Hazel's plane had gone down looked miles away. It'd be a mighty struggle getting there and finding our friend.

I crammed the canteen, the first-aid kit, and a rolled-up blanket into an empty canvas bag.

"I'm ready," I said, throwing the bag over my shoulder. "Let's . . . Wait a minute."

I sank to my knees.

"What ya doin'?" Leo demanded, gathering his rope and tying it to his belt.

I ignored him and finished. When I stood up, I said, "Praying for Hazel."

He looked at me like he thought I'd lost my mind. But he said nothing.

Leo led us down the mesa. At the base, I couldn't tell which direction to go. "Those trees . . . I can't see."

"Just follow me, gal," he replied.

We set out across the level, rocky plain. The trees began a good ways off, maybe an hour's hike. Above, the sun began to heat up the morning.

As I trotted along, I pictured Hazel trapped in the crashed plane or lying injured beside it. I could almost hear her groaning in pain. I shut my eyes, hoping the awful pictures and imagined sounds would go away.

Then I forced those images out of my head by remembering how she'd helped me just a few weeks ago. When I

crossed the country looking for Mama and Daddy, she'd
rescued me after an awful flood. I'd been sick and Hazel
took me to her home in Flagstaff and nursed me. Later,
when I got kidnapped by a vile cuss, Hazel had flown her
plane all over, searching me out. She was a true enough
hero to my mind. I loved her as I would my own kin. We
had to find her fast and help her. We just *had* to.

By the time we reached the forest, the sun had climbed
high in the sky. I felt its warmth on my back, but it
brought no comfort. We darted through the trees in silence, my thoughts churning, fearful for Hazel.

"Leo, do you think Hazel is . . . OK?" I asked.

"Yep," he replied, not even turning to look at me.

"Leo, tell me true," I insisted. "I won't be lied to."

He stopped and spun around, his dark eyes wide.
"What do ya want me to say, gal? That she's fine and
dandy after just crashin' that blasted contraption?"

Yes. That was exactly what I wanted to hear. Not the
truth at all.

"Well, I just dunno," he went on. Then his eyes
clouded up, and he turned away from me. "You could
crash a plane and walk away from it or you could crash
and—"

He didn't finish. Instead, he tramped on through the
woods. Following, I tried to leave Hazel in God's hands.
But I silently pleaded with Him not to take her away.

We'd been going a while when Leo halted. He stooped
down to the ground and rubbed his stubby fingers across
the dirt.

"What are you doing?" I asked.

Without looking at me, he answered, "Something mighty strange here, gal."

"What?"

"Take a lookit them tracks," he said, pointing at the ground.

I knelt beside him. In the dirt I spied two wide prints. They didn't look like the tracks of a horse or anything I'd ever seen before.

"What kind of animal would leave tracks like that?"

"Dunno," Leo admitted. "Not bear or mountain lion. Too big for a wolf." He gazed at me. "I jest sure hope we don't run into it—whatever it is."

* * *

I couldn't get a fix on the sun, so I didn't know how long we'd been marching through the towering pines. It seemed like forever. But at least we saw no more strange animal tracks. And better yet, no strange animals.

Suddenly, broken tree limbs cluttered our path.

Leo turned around. "We're gittin' close," he said, his eyes fearful.

I frowned at him. "How do you know?"

He just said, "Use your nose. And your eyes."

Then he took off running.

"Leo!" Goodness, what—I looked at the broken tree limbs. I sniffed the air.

At once I recognized the smell. Smoke! I remembered

the wisp of black smoke curling into the sky. And the
limbs—knocked down as the airplane crashed through the
trees!

"Leo!" I screamed.

I chased after him, leaping over mounds of moss-cov-
ered rock and weaving between the densely growing
pines.

"Wait up, Leo!" I shouted. I caught sight of his red
shirt and raced after it.

Gasping for air, I tried to catch up. Soon I smelled something heavy and oily. Every breath I took choked me.

Then, just when I thought I'd lost him, I ran right into
Leo. He stood at the edge of a small clearing. His shoulders heaved as he struggled to catch his breath.

"For goodness sake—" I began.

But my eyes gazed beyond my friend and fixed on
something in the clearing.

A ragged piece of the airplane's tail lay splintered on
the carpet of pine needles right in front of me. I pushed
past Leo and stumbled toward it. *Dear God!* My heart
pounded and the most awful thoughts crashed in my head.
Dear God, I pleaded, *please let Hazel be all right. Please!* I
reached out and touched the crunched metal. Then my
eyes drifted up and I saw other pieces of the plane.

High above us, wrapped around the trunk of a tree like
a ragged shawl, I spied one of the Waco's wings. Bits of
red dotted the trees as if they were bleeding. Splintered
chunks of pine hung limp where the plane had crashed
through them.

"No!" I shouted at this forest. *"No!"*

"Gal . . ." Leo began but left off. There were no words of comfort.

A memory sprang into my mind. The morning after a tornado when we lived in Oklahoma. It had swept around our little tenant farmhouse and picked up and dropped the strangest things. Out in the yard we found an upright piano. Lois Jester's, we came to discover. Plucked up from her house and dropped on our land. But in the trees north of our fields I had discovered something awful. Dozens of dead birds caught in the limbs of the scrub oaks. The scene had struck me with its eerie silence. No birds chirped that morning. Or for many mornings after that.

And for the first time I noticed the unnatural silence around us. No birds chirped in this clearing either.

After a minute my mind came back to Hazel. To finding her fast! I set out following the path of the plane through the trees. I ran hard, leaving Leo behind. My arms and legs pumped furiously and with what breath I could manage, I called out, *"Hazel! Hazel! Where are you?"*

My breathing roared in my ears as I ran. Other pieces of the Waco lay about, but I didn't stop. I had to find the part with the seats. What did Hazel call it? I couldn't think. I figured Hazel would still be with that section, buckled in tight. Kept safe.

I spotted the propeller sunk deep in a tree trunk, stabbing it like an arrow shot from a bow. A wheel lay at the base of another tree. Here and there I came across more parts of the plane.

Then, finally, I spied it. The fuselage — that's what she called it. It looked intact, though strange without the wings and tail. Throwing the canvas bag to the ground, I raced to it.

But when I reached the cockpit, where I'd seen Hazel wave to me before she took off, I discovered only an empty seat.

My friend, Hazel Womack, was gone.

Chapter 9

If it's true that blood can run cold, then mine did at that moment. I commenced to shivering so bad my teeth chattered. Could it be that this fine lady and true friend had completely disappeared?

"Leo, she's gone!" I exclaimed.

I feared the crash had yanked Hazel right out of the plane and thrown her like a rag doll through the forest. But when I studied the inside of the cockpit, I saw the seat belt undone and laying neatly on the seat. Maybe Hazel had climbed out on her own. I should have been relieved. But still I fretted: what if Hazel had forgotten to buckle her seat belt?

Leo examined the cockpit. "Bet Hazel's OK," he said. "Probably she's headed back toward the pueblo."

His calm gave me a faint hope. Hazel could still be somewhere in the forest.

"Hazel!" I sang out at once. "Hazel, where are you?"

Leo picked it up too, and we wandered in different directions, calling out her name.

No answer.

She didn't seem to be anywhere nearby. Or if she was,

she couldn't hear. Or if she could hear, she couldn't answer. I grew frightened again.

"We've got to get help," I decided aloud. "We've got to find her and get her to the doctor."

"But which way do you reckon help is?" Leo said, his dark eyes now tense with worry.

"Hazel told us Cal Maddox's ranch is somewhere around here," I said.

"Maddox?" he cried. "That mean ol' cuss from yesterday?"

"He may be a mean cuss, but he can't be totally without feelings," I replied. "And there's his daughter, Areana. I'm sure she'd help us. But how'll we ever find his ranch?"

Leo's face scrunched up. He got that pained look I'd seen before when he thought on a thing real hard. Then he smiled and untied the leather thong holding his rope to his belt.

"I'll climb one of these here trees, gal," he declared. "Then maybe I'll be able to see which way to go."

"Good idea, Leo!"

He chose what he figured to be the tallest tree. Then he made a lasso and roped a limb to pull himself up on. In seconds he climbed to the limb and started up. As he called out his progress up the tree, I took another look around.

I came upon a piece of wing tightly wrapped around the trunk of a pine. Goodness! What would the force of a crashing plane do to a person thrown from it? I shook the awful answer from my mind. Hazel just had to be all right. I had to trust God to protect her. But where would He put her to keep her safe?

After a while, Leo yelled out high above me, "I'm all the way up! I can't see— Wait! Somethin' off thataway!"

I stared up into the tree. I couldn't even see his red shirt, much less the direction he meant.

Suddenly, I heard something drop through the limbs. *Leo!* But no. I saw at once it wasn't my friend. A small object landed and bounced on the soft carpet of pine needles. I raced over to it.

A shoe! I plucked it up and examined it. It belonged to Leo all right. The leather had worn badly. I poked my finger through a hole in the sole, pushing up the scrap of cardboard he'd tucked inside to protect the bottom of his foot. I reminded myself to tell Mama this poor boy sorely needed a new pair of shoes.

High above me Leo called out, "Don't move the shoe, *gal!* That's our compass!"

Compass? How could a shoe be a compass? But I laid it down in the spot where it had landed and waited for him to climb down.

After a bit, I caught sight of his red shirt. Then I spotted the rest of him, including a shoeless foot sporting a brown sock with a hole in the toe.

Finally, he undid the lasso from the limb, dropped the rope, and shinnied down the trunk of the tree.

"Whew!" he huffed, brushing bits of bark from his clothes.

"What did you see?" I asked as I picked pine needles from his hair.

"Where'd my shoe land?"

"Over there," I told him, pointing.

We headed in that direction.

"I spotted a fancy looking gate off that way," he said. "That's why I threw my shoe. So I wouldn't get confused which way to go when I climbed down."

"Leo, you truly amaze me," I declared.

He smiled then looked away, like he didn't know what to make of such words. He sat on the ground and pulled on his shoe.

"How'll we find our way back here?" I asked him.

"Gal, you're gonna hafta learn some tricks if you hope to survive in the woods," he told me. "Stay here."

He ran off. Survive in the woods? I sure didn't count on needing to know such things. I planned to get *out* of the woods.

When he returned, he held a small piece of metal from the wreckage.

"This'll do," he announced. "Got a ragged end on it sharp enough to scratch up a tree some."

I picked up the canvas bag, and we ran in the direction he'd seen the gate. As we hurried, Leo scratched a line in the bark of a tree every so often. Marking our trail. That Leo had some head on his shoulders!

The way out of the forest seemed to take forever. Dodging this way and that, I wondered about Hazel. Where could she be? I tried to convince myself she was all right. But then I thought of that plane, all ripped to pieces. How could anyone be all right after a crash like that? My mind drifted from one dreadful thing to another.

Finally, we reached the edge of the forest. In the west, the setting sun had turned the sky red and purple. The air became crisp and cool. Off in the distance I made out what Leo had seen from atop the tree. A broad, metal gate glittered in the sunset. A dirt road led through the gate and beyond.

Leo raced across the dusty ground toward the gate. I felt plumb worn out, but I struggled to keep up with him.

When we reached the gate, I collapsed against it. I felt I couldn't go a step farther. I gulped in some air and gazed up at the shiny metal gate. Above our heads I spied in fancy letters a single word:

Silverado

This had to be Cal Maddox's ranch!

"Come on," I said after I caught my breath.

Leo didn't argue. We climbed over the gate and headed up the dirt road as fast as we could manage.

The road led over a hill and then wound around a rocky outcrop. Here only a few trees dotted the land. We stopped only to drink from the canteen.

The sun disappeared behind a ridge and it grew dark quickly. We kept going. Then we saw lights in the distance.

"That's it!" I cried. "Let's go!"

"Gal, I can't," complained Leo. "I feel like my innards are on fire."

"You can do it," I insisted, my thoughts fixed on Hazel. "Come on!"

I ran hard, my legs and arms pumping. My lungs ached with each breath. But I kept going. I heard Leo panting behind me.

Even in the dark the house looked big. It stretched out long and low. In a shadowy part of the wide porch the dark shape of a porch swing swayed. Light poured from the windows and lit up a patch of the yard. I saw two cars parked there. Cal Maddox's and Areana's. They were home!

At last, we stumbled up the porch steps and collapsed.

"G-gal, d-don't never make me run that far again," Leo wheezed. He lay across the steps in a heap.

I forced myself up and staggered toward the front door. Through the window I spied Areana. Thank You, God! I just knew she'd help us find Hazel.

Before I could knock, a quick movement near the porch swing caught my eye. A dark shadow rose up, seeming to expand and grow. Then the shadow reached out and grabbed my arm. I felt the powerful strength of its grip on me.

My eyes darted back to the window. Areana was gone.

"What do you want?" a deep voice boomed.

The shadow stepped into the light, but I already knew that voice.

It belonged to none other than Cal Maddox himself.

Chapter 10

Being grabbed unexpected-like put the fright in me. I pretty much froze to the spot. But something about his dark shadow made my mind jump back to last night. Could Cal Maddox be the phantom?

"I said, 'What do you want?' " Maddox repeated in his deep, rough voice.

All the fright and weariness went out of me then. Phantom or no phantom, I had to get help.

"It's Hazel," I cried. "Her plane crashed in the forest. We went there, but we couldn't fi—"

"*Hazel,* you say?" Maddox interrupted. "What happened? Her plane crashed?"

I thought I heard worry in his words. So I said, "Yessir. In the forest back there."

"Did you search for her?"

"Yessir. We found the plane—broken up and all. But no sign of Hazel."

"*Thunderation!*" he exclaimed. "We must find her at once." Whatever he'd held against Hazel seemed to have vanished.

Leo got up and joined me.

"I marked the way," he announced.

"Better go then," Maddox insisted. He grabbed his white cowboy hat from the porch swing. Then, leading me by the arm, he rushed us down the steps toward the car.

"What about your daughter?" I said. "Shouldn't you tell her you're leaving?"

Maddox didn't answer. He opened the front car door and shoved me, then Leo, inside. He climbed in beside us.

At once the noisy vehicle took off down the dirt road toward the gate. Inside the car, the engine's roar made my head hurt and my teeth rattle. I held my hands over my ears, but it didn't help. Daddy would've considered this a car in desperate need of attention.

Maddox's voice exploded over the noise of the engine, "How come you two weren't in that plane with Hazel?"

I yelled back, "She'd set off for supplies. She only planned to be gone a short time."

When we reached the gate to the ranch, Maddox slammed on the brakes.

"Which way?" he demanded.

Leo pointed toward the trees. Maddox tromped the gas pedal and the car shot off the road and up a slope toward the forest.

He steered like he spoke—with violence. His elbows came up as he worked the steering wheel. Twice he jabbed Leo hard. My friend leaned against me, and I pressed against the door to give Maddox room.

I glanced at the man. The lights from the dashboard glowed green in his face, making him look like some kind of monster. But he was no monster, I told myself. He must be a true friend to Hazel, willing to risk his very vehicle to get to her in her time of need.

As the car plowed into the forest, my gaze darted to the windshield. We plunged through that forest with a fury, dodging first one tree then another. Land o' Goshen, as Hazel would say. I wanted to hide my eyes but I couldn't. I just stared out the windshield, as if watching for exactly which tree would be the end of us.

Leo pointed at the scrape marks he'd made on the trees. "There's one!" he'd cry. "And another!" But how Maddox managed to see them at this speed, and with the car's headlights bouncing all over the place, I couldn't figure.

Finally, the forest proved too dense for even Maddox and his frantic driving. He'd dodge one tree only to skid into another. All the while we bounced wildly over the rocky ground. When a row of sturdy pines stood like a wall in front of us, the rancher slammed on his brakes. The vehicle skidded across the pine needles, stopping just short of a massive tree.

"Thunderation!" he spat at the forest, as if it had defeated him. "We'll have to hoof it from here."

We climbed out of the car and Maddox retrieved a flashlight from under the seat. Then from the backseat he grabbed a green canvas rucksack. I realized suddenly that I'd left our pack on Maddox's porch.

"Let's go," Maddox commanded.

We set out through the trees with Maddox leading. I guessed we didn't move fast enough for him because he shouted, "Get a move on, you two. Gotta find her!"

I admired his concern for Hazel, so I put aside his gruff manner. Leo and I hurried after him, barely able to keep up. Maddox walked with a fury.

He didn't even wait for Leo's help finding the scuffed trees. He plunged on through the forest.

"Hazel Womack!" he yelled. "Where are you, woman?"

Before long we reached the first scraps of wrecked plane. Maddox's light fell on the broken wing, and I stopped dead still. Seeing the wreckage again gave me a prickly feeling that crept up and down my arms and at the back of my neck. I felt a little sick to my stomach. Dear Lord, where was Hazel?

Then Leo and I joined Maddox in calling out for her. Our shouts filled the forest. But no one answered.

"Maybe she wasn't hurt bad," I suggested to Cal Maddox. "Maybe she got up and walked off to find us."

"From *this?*" Maddox replied. He shined his light at the debris around us. "No one could walk away from—"

At that instant his light found the fuselage. The rancher shoved past Leo and me and ran for it. We followed after him though back a ways. Nothing seemed changed, except the darkness made it creepier.

Light in hand, Maddox examined every corner of the cockpit, as if Hazel could be hiding in there somewhere. Then he went to the two forward seats and shined the light around for a long time. It hit me all at once. Maddox was searching for something all right. But I doubted it was Hazel.

"Thunderation," he said.

He swung the light to the ground again and rushed from one chunk of wreckage to another. Leo and I stayed put.

I spoke softly to my friend, "I think we ought to get out of here."

"You reckon?"

"Look at the man, Leo," I whispered. "He's not looking for Hazel. He's after—"

At that moment Maddox's light shone right in my face. My hands flew up to cover my eyes.

"Get that light out of my eyes," I told Maddox.

I heard the stomp of his boots coming my way. Leo muttered, "Uh-oh."

Then I felt Maddox's large hand around my arm, gripping it tight.

"Unhand me," I told him. I was plenty afraid of the man, but I wouldn't let him see it. "Let me go."

The light went away and I heard Leo shout, "Lemme go! You got no call to—"

"Listen here, you two, I'll not be tricked," Maddox boomed. "The last person who crossed Caleb Maddox regretted it to his dying day."

I tugged, trying to free my arm from his grasp. He held on tighter.

"There's no trick here," I said. "You can see for yourself what happened."

"I can see that Hazel's nowhere about," he growled. "And I can see that chest isn't about either."

Another icy chill swept through me.

"What chest?" I said.

"The chest you found," he answered. "I saw it yesterday morning. Then last night it was gone. I figure Hazel
hid it in that plane, all set to sneak it off to Flagstaff."

I stared at the dark shape of Cal Maddox and began to
understand. He'd played some part in the strange goings
on last night in the pueblo. He and Areana.

"You were after that chest last night," I said. "And I'll
bet you stole our food."

"Better for you if I'd found the chest," he said flatly. "I
took that food so you'd all clear out."

"And you were blowing that flute," I accused. "And
running around with Areana in the pueblo."

"I don't know what you're talking about," he spat.

I yanked my arm something fierce. "Let me go, you
vile man!"

Suddenly he shoved Leo and me hard against the ground.
"I want the truth outta you upstarts," he declared hotly.
"The chest—where is it?"

He shone the flashlight first in my face, then in Leo's.
Neither of us spoke a word.

I heard Maddox fiddling with his rucksack. His flashlight
lay on the ground. In its light I caught a glimpse of something. Something dreadful. The dark outline of a pistol.

Maddox's voice thundered, seeming to shake the trees
around us.

"All right, you two. You wouldn't come looking for me
if Hazel hadn't put you up to it. I know a trick when I see
it. I want that chest. And I want it now."

Chapter 11

In that dark forest, with Maddox standing over us and holding a pistol, I grew truly frightened. But in spite of my fear, I didn't want to tell Maddox where I thought the chest might be. It didn't belong to him.

"He's crazy, gal," Leo whispered in my ear. "Can't trust 'im."

"Get up, you upstarts, right now!" Maddox ordered.

I leaned close and whispered, "Maybe we can make a run for it."

"Huh? With him holdin' that *gun?*" Leo whispered back.

"Get up, I said!" Maddox cried, kicking my shoe with his shiny-tipped boot.

I rose up then, feeling pretty furious myself. "You've no call to go kicking me or shoving me around," I told him. "If you'd treat folks better, you might enjoy life some."

"Spare me the words of wisdom," Maddox huffed. "I want that chest *now.*"

Leo stood up beside me. His hand lightly grasped my arm. I had to do something to buy us some time, so I could work out some sort of plan.

"All right, you win," I said. "Come on, Leo, let's show him where we hid the chest." I nudged Leo good so he'd keep still.

If we could only get that flashlight, then we might have a chance to escape. Unless he were part cat, he couldn't see in the dark any better than we could.

"We'll need your flashlight," I said. "It's off thataway"—I pointed in some direction—"but we can't find it blind."

I reached for the flashlight, but he jerked it away. "I'll tend the light," he said firmly. "You just go ahead."

So much for getting the light.

As Leo and I picked our way through the dark, I kept hoping a plan would pop into my head. But nothing came to me save to wait and watch for a chance to run. Maddox pointed the light over our shoulders, making a yellow oval on the forest floor. Suddenly, I felt Leo's hand clasp mine tight. I looked hard at him. In the bright light sweeping past our heads and shoulders I saw him nod down to his side. He patted the rope coiled at his belt.

Heroic notions! That boy and his rope had gotten us out of a real fix back in California when we stood face to face with a wolf on Will Rogers' ranch. Now he planned to play cowboy all over again. And with Maddox every bit as dangerous as any wolf.

I kept going, afraid to say anything to Leo for fear Maddox would hear. You just can't stop a boy from doing the most fool thing once he sets his mind on it. Maybe Leo's plan would work. I hoped to heaven it would.

If Maddox could tell my intention was to lead him on a

wild goose chase, he didn't let on. He kept traipsing after
me with that light pointed over my shoulder. But I knew
he'd soon get his fill of my wanderings. Then what would
I do?

Leo nudged me. I saw out of the corner of my eye that
he'd freed his rope from his belt and he gripped it in his
left hand.

After a bit Maddox complained, "This better be the
way, you little upstart, or you'll be plenty sorry."

"It's just up ahead," I said, trying to sound cheery, like
we were on a Sunday picnic. But my heart didn't feel
cheery. And this was no picnic.

I saw Leo fashioning a small lasso.

Then, in one terrible second, I saw the lasso drop to
the ground. *Oh no!* I looked at Leo. But in the beam of
light I could see his smile. Had he meant to drop it? I also
saw he still held the other end of the rope.

"Hold it!" barked Maddox.

Oh no! He must have seen the lasso drop to the
ground.

We stopped dead still but didn't turn.

"I don't know what kind of fool you take me for," he
began. I expected him to fetch up the lasso and fix us
good. "I know you're leading me back to that blasted
pueblo. Is that where you hid the chest?"

Toward the pueblo? I figured we were just going in
circles.

"Um, yessir, that's where it is all right," I said, still
facing away from him.

"You saying it wasn't in the plane after all?" he demanded.

"Nosir," I replied truthfully. "Just Hazel. Headed for Flagstaff for supplies."

His laugh cracked through the trees like limbs breaking. "Whatta you take me for?"

I turned and dimly saw the lasso laying on the ground just in front of Maddox's feet. Leo planned to trip the man! But there'd be no tripping him unless we could get him to step into the circle of rope.

"Come back here," ordered Maddox, his feet planted to the spot.

I thought quickly. I had to get him to take another step forward. I clutched Leo's sleeve and tugged backward. Then I took a step back.

"No, I don't think I'll do that," I declared.

Maddox raised the pistol. I saw it shimmer in the light. "You'd better."

I took another step back. Then another.

"Stay put, upstart," he warned.

I stepped back again. Leo backed up beside me.

Then Maddox stepped forward. Leo yanked hard on the rope. It came up taut around Maddox's boot.

"Whoa!" the rancher cried out. The light shot up toward the trees as Maddox stumbled to the ground.

"Run, Leo!" I yelled.

We dropped the rope and raced off.

Behind us, Maddox shouted, "Come back here, you upstarts! *Come back here!"*

We fled through the darkness, dodging trees. Leo led the way and I held tight to his shirttail. Low limbs slapped our faces, but we kept running, fleeing the crazed rancher. It didn't take long to get plumb worn out.

When I couldn't run any farther, I collapsed on the ground, pulling Leo down after me. There we lay, gasping for air.

I listened for Maddox but heard nothing. Only our panting as we tried to catch our breath.

"Did we ... really get away from him?" I finally managed to say.

"Near as I ... can figure," Leo gasped. "Gosh, gal, he's ... one bad cowpoke."

"He is that," I agreed.

My legs ached so bad I wanted to lie on the ground forever. But I knew better. Maddox wouldn't stand for a couple of mere children getting the best of him. He'd be coming after us. And soon.

I forced myself up. "We gotta keep going."

"Where?"

A good question. We couldn't hope to find Hazel in the dark. And finding the pueblo would be tricky too. We'd probably spend the whole night wandering the forest.

"We can't stay here," I said.

I turned around, trying to spy something, a direction we could go, a hiding place. I made out a large, dark mound. I reached down and pulled Leo to his feet.

"Come on, let's hide over there."

He let me lead. We picked our way around some trees

toward the mound.

"What is this thing?" he said.

"A pile of rock and earth, I guess."

We walked around it. Scratchy, waist-high brush grew there, which would hide us better than a clump of trees.

"We'd best lay low till first light, then find the way outta here," Leo said.

It made sense to me. So we sank down on the ground in the midst of the brush. I'd slept outside plenty before, but the cool air made me shiver. Just like it had last night when I set out chasing that phantom. This trip had turned out a whole lot different from what I'd expected. First the mysterious phantom. Then Cal Maddox. And Hazel, dear, poor Hazel. What about her?

I wished at that moment I was tucked in bed at home with Mama and Daddy sleeping peacefully in the next room. If only—

Just then came the sound of footsteps in the underbrush. I sat up at once, alert. I thought, *Surely not. Surely*— Then a sudden, awful glare flashed in our faces. And worst of all the voice. The booming, vile growl of the man we thought we had escaped.

"All right, upstarts. On your feet. You'll not play me for a fool twice. You're mine now. All mine."

Chapter 12

I couldn't see the villain's face with the flashlight beam blinding me. But I saw in my mind the hard lines, the scowl. I figured he had his pistol in hand, aimed right at us.

"Get up, you upstarts," he commanded.

Leo whispered, "Do what he says, gal."

We had no choice. I got to my feet and pulled Leo up with me.

"All right, where's it at?" Maddox said. "Tell me now. I won't tolerate any more foolishness."

I swallowed and made myself answer. "If you're talking about that chest, we don't know. We don't know where Hazel is either. We told you before. The plane crashed and we looked for Hazel but never found her."

"You expect me to believe that?" came Maddox's reply.

"It's the truth," I told him.

I could hear him breathing hard, like he was struggling to keep from exploding. The sound scared me what with not being able to see him and all. But my impatience with the man's rudeness finally overcame my fear.

"Kindly turn that light away from our faces," I said.

"You might be doing serious damage to our eyes."

"You're a tart little thing, aren't you?"

"I'm not a thing. I'm a person. And worth decent treatment."

Gradually the light eased down a bit. Thank goodness!

We listened to Maddox breathing again. With the light aimed down, I could see a bit of our surroundings. This mound of earth—what was it?

"What exactly did you find in that chest?" Maddox asked.

I waited a moment, but I couldn't think what harm there'd be in telling him. Maybe the contents wouldn't interest him and he'd just let us go. Maybe . . .

"Tell me," he thundered. "I know you looked inside."

"Hazel called them Spanish artifacts," I said. "Just some old trinkets. A goblet of some sort. A handful of old coins. A Spanish stirrup—"

"Yes, yes," he broke in impatiently. "I'm sure of all that. But what of—well, *documents?* You see anything with writing on it?"

"Such as a book?"

"Such as a book, yes, or, well, a map."

A map! So that was it. I read the heart of the man at once. He coveted a different treasure, not old worn copper coins, not stirrups. Something else.

"Didn't see a map," I said, speaking the honest truth.

"What about you, boy?" Maddox said. "Did you see a map in that chest?"

"I didn't see no map 'tall," Leo snapped. "Why don't

you just be on about your business and leave us alone?"

Worthy Leo! He'd been plenty brave facing that California wolf. Now he'd proved himself worthy before this Arizona fox.

"No map!" Maddox's voice boomed. "How can that be? You're lying to me. I won't have it! You hear me?"

His words stung me. Stung me sharp, like salt biting into an open wound.

"You're a rude man, Cal Maddox," I snapped back. "You'd do well to go home. Your own daughter doesn't even know your whereabouts."

There came the sound of him breathing again. In a moment it stopped. He seemed to mull over my words.

More softly he asked, "You sure there was no map?"

Since he turned civil, I decided to answer him civil. "No sir, no map. Just what I told you, along with some trinkets I didn't recognize. All wrapped up in an animal skin of some sort."

I heard him suck in his breath sharply.

"Animal skin!" he cried. "That's it!"

At first his words made no sense. I feared the man had gone full crazy. Then I recalled the black markings etched on the animal skin in the chest. Could that have been his precious map?

Leo tugged me backward. Another cowboy escape plan! But Maddox had his eyes fixed on us.

"Stand firm there, you upstarts," he ordered. "I'll not have you slip off from me again. So don't even try."

The beam from the flashlight held us trapped.

"Got to find that chest," Maddox mumbled. "But I don't trust you two. *Say,* what have we here?"

The light darted to the mound of earth. For the first time I noticed a dark opening in the mound, like a doorway.

Maddox's laugh thundered in the night like a wild animal's roar. The sound chilled me right to the bone. I felt I was in the presence of something terrible, something vile. *Dear God,* I said to myself, *help us now.*

"The old mine," Maddox said. "A good enough place to store the likes of you."

He shoved us backward.

"Hey, watch it!" shouted Leo.

"No complaints from you, boy," the rancher warned. "And you'll get no help from your blasted rope either. It's mine now." I saw him wave the coiled rope.

He backed us into the mouth of the mine. I breathed in its odor. It smelled old and musty and rotten.

"Just what do you want?" I asked the man. "You think that map'll make you richer?"

Maddox didn't answer.

"More gold, more silver?" I said as he gave us another push. The three of us stooped inside the opening now. I pictured Cal Maddox's silver-toed boots, the shiny tips of his collar, his bold, silver ring. The gate to his ranch—Silverado. "Silver, that's it, isn't it? You hunger for silver."

He shoved us back again. The stale air sickened me. So different from the pleasant smell of earth being tilled, like

Daddy used to do back in Oklahoma before the dust
storms came. This odor made me gag.

"Ain't nothing wrong loving things of beauty,"
Maddox's voice echoed around us. "Can't hold that
against me. Silver's got a rich luster all its own. You look
into it and it draws you in. Almost spiritual, it is."

The man's words offended me even more than his
harsh manner.

I said, "You can't go seeking things of the spirit in
silver and such."

Maddox grabbed my arm. He leaned close and asked,
"You one of them religious gals?"

"I'm a Christian, Mr. Maddox," I declared. "And I
know the truth—that Jesus is more precious than silver
or gold."

"Don't know about Jesus," Maddox said, "but I never
much cared for gold."

As Maddox took another step toward us, Leo cried out,
"I can't go no farther. Somethin's blockin' the way."

Maddox's light revealed an object behind Leo.

"Well, well," the rancher said.

At first it appeared to be a large, rusted metal box. But
when the light picked up the wheels and the track underneath, I understood at once. It was an old mine car. Min-
ers would shove it down the track which descended like a
hill into the depths of the mine. Then they'd load the car
with ore and haul it out by pulling it back up the track.

"Get in there," Maddox told us.

"What?" I said.

"You heard me. I said 'get in there.' *Now.*"

"I'd like to know your intentions first," I said.

"You're the sassiest thing."

I crossed my arms. "I may appear sassy to you, but you seem bent on doing us ill. I'll not willingly throw myself into danger. And if you think otherwise, you don't know who you're dealing with."

I heard a long sigh.

Then I felt the sharp jab of the gun barrel against my arm. "I know I'm dealing with pure mule stubbornness," Maddox said. "You'd best climb into that mine car with your little buddy before you regret it."

The gun against my arm convinced me. I didn't think he'd shoot a child, but I figured it best not to tempt him.

Leo climbed over first. Then he reached out and helped me. When I jumped down inside, my shoes thudded against the car's bottom. Inside, the car felt grimy and rough. When Maddox shined his light in, I saw rusty flakes peeling away.

"Stand back to back, upstarts," Maddox ordered. "No more lip from either of you. Do as I say."

At once I felt a circle of rope come down over us, then cinch us tight together. My arms were pinned at my sides. Leaning into the car, Maddox then wrapped the rest of the rope around us, tying it off.

"There you go," he said. "That oughta keep you."

"What do you mean to do with us?" Leo demanded.

"I mean to keep you out of the way while I find out where Hazel hid my chest."

"Your chest?" I asked.

"It should be mine," he replied. "I studied all about it. About the sixteenth-century Spanish expedition down south. About the silver they found. About the map."

"But that doesn't make it yours," I declared.

"I'll not waste my time addressing the likes of you," he bellowed. "Now get cozy. By the time you get loose, I'll have what I want."

Then his light swung away. In the darkness I heard his heavy footsteps tramping off. Soon only dark silence surrounded us. We were trapped!

"Why is it, gal, since I met you I keep gettin' tied up in dark places?" Leo asked.

He was referring to how we'd been tied up together in an old horse trailer when we tried to find Will Rogers' stolen horse. In that adventure, he'd managed to work loose our bindings after much twisting and squirming.

"We can get free," I told him. "Maddox probably had his mind on silver, not knots."

We wiggled this way and that trying to loosen the rope. As it turned out, Maddox'd tied us up good. He'd knotted the rope at our feet, out of reach. As we struggled against each other, the old mine car bounced up and down. Our stomping feet made a strange echoing drumbeat in the dark. Finally, I felt one of the ropes loosen a little.

"Jump again!" I exclaimed. "I can move my hand."

We jumped hard and lost our balance, falling to the floor of the car. A thunderous boom echoed in the mine. The car creaked and rocked on the track.

"What was that?" Leo asked.

"What was what?" I replied.

"Did you feel the mine car rock?"

"A little. We're on wheels on a track, Leo. It's bound to rock some. Come on, let's get up and jump again."

"Gal, I don't know . . ."

I didn't understand his worry. We wanted to get free, didn't we? And jumping seemed to help work the ropes loose.

We struggled back to our feet. Balanced together, we jumped again. And again. Each time the mine car rocked a little. Maybe the rusty old thing would fall apart.

"Keep jumping," I insisted. "My hand's almost loose."

We kept after it. Then . . .

BLAM!

We crashed to the floor of the mine car. My breath flew out of me. I lay there stunned.

"It worked, gal!" Leo said, yanking his arm free.

With my face pressed up against the side of the car, I felt something funny. A slight movement. A vibration.

Oh, no. Dear God, no.

Suddenly Leo pushed hard against me, kicking his legs. "I'm loose, gal!" he cried.

"No, Leo, *don't move!*"

"What?"

I tried to lie perfectly still, but it did no good.

The mine car creaked into motion. In a moment it began rolling down the track!

"Whoa!" Leo shouted as the mine car plunged down, down, down into the black heart of the mine.

Chapter 13

"Yeeeeooooowwwwwwww!"

We screamed as we plunged deeper, and faster, into the mine. As the car shot down, a loud scraping noise rang out. How I wanted my hands free to clap over my ears!

Leo and I huddled in the corner of the boxy car.

"Dear Father in heaven," I started to pray, but the speed and the scraping sound sickened me. I couldn't think, let alone pray.

Rocking back and forth, the car raced faster. Faster!

An awful thought hit me. Where would this track end? I tried to look around, but only blackness surrounded us.

With Leo free, I pulled the loose ropes from me. All the while the mine car rocketed down the track.

"Gotta stop it!" I cried.

Faster and faster the car careened down the track. My heart pounded. My head pounded too. I pressed myself back into the corner. Leo sat close and I gripped his hand. What on earth would become of us?

"Where do mine tracks end?" I cried out.

"Where they stopped minin'," Leo called back.

I held his hand tighter. What would Mama and Daddy think, losing their only daughter, and their only "almost son," in some abandoned mine in Arizona?

Crazy, crazy thoughts sped through my mind as the car sped along the track.

Then something happened. The track must have leveled out because the car slowed some.

"It's stopping," I shouted.

"Not yet," Leo shot back.

We stuck our heads up. The awful creaking had quieted a little, but another strange sound struck my ears.

"What's that?" I said.

He knew at once what I meant. "Sounds different. Maybe it's—Oh my goodness!"

"What?"

"The end of the line!" he hollered.

"Get down!" I cried, yanking him.

I braced myself and held tight. Then—

CRASH!

We pitched forward, slamming hard against the other side of the mine car. *Ow!* Then the car toppled over, throwing Leo and me out. I lay there stunned. Leo groaned beside me. Before I could move or speak, a tremendous roar filled my ears. Dust caught in my throat. I could scarcely breathe.

The roar grew louder and louder. Then a cascade of pebbles showered our heads. Something told me to move—to get back into the overturned car. Still shaky, I felt around for Leo and pulled on him.

"Come on!" I gasped.

He seemed groggy. I kept yanking on him as I crawled back to the mine car.

"Hurry!" I urged, pulling him in after me.

Then it happened. The ceiling of the mine came crashing down around us.

Chapter 14

We lay there awhile. A good long while. Dust clouded up around us, and we both commenced to coughing something awful. Every so often, another ripple of rock and debris came trickling down like dusty hailstones, pinging on the side of the overturned mine car.

When the dust settled, I crawled out. Thanks to God, the car had protected us. I felt around. Most of the rock must have fallen behind us, on the other side of the car.

My body seemed one big ache. Still, I struggled to my feet, holding on to the mine car for support. When I stood, my head bumped something above me and set off another hail of dirt and pebbles. I felt the ceiling. It seemed higher in some parts. Because, I guessed, part of it had just crashed down on us.

As I breathed in, I commenced coughing again. When it eased up, I reached down and pulled Leo up beside me.

"What *(cough cough cough cough)* happened?" he wheezed.

"A *(cough cough cough)* cave-in," I managed to say. Talking only made me cough worse.

I remembered the dust storms back in Liberal, Kansas

where I'd lived with my aunt and her family. So I fetched
out my bandanna from my overalls pocket and tied it over
my nose and mouth. Leo carried a bandanna himself, and
he dug it out of his pants pocket and tied it like mine.

"Well, we stopped," he said, sounding exhausted.

"Sit down and rest, boy," I ordered. I remembered
something. "Give me those matches you've got."

I left him beside the mine car and felt my way around.
The rough rock felt cool to my touch. And solid. And
immovable. In the dark space, I smacked my head twice
against the low ceiling. I struck a match and took a look
around. It burned down to my fingers and I dropped it. I
struck another. It didn't take me long to realize that what
I feared had come true.

"What you doin', gal?" Leo croaked.

"Finding out what happened," I told him.

"Yeah, and ... ?"

I forced myself not to cry. I didn't want to frighten Leo.
But I choked on the words as I said them: "The cave-in
happened right behind the mine car." I bit my lip, keeping
myself from screaming. "We're trapped."

"We can jest go out the way we come in." He spoke as
if he didn't catch my meaning.

"The way's blocked. We're in a little rock room."

A gasp came from his direction. *"Can't be!"* he cried.
"Gotta be a way out!"

I heard him stumble around the mine car, muttering to
himself. I followed his voice and the sound of him clawing
at the rock wall.

"Jest *gotta* be a way out!" he gasped. "Gotta be."

"Leo," I said, reaching out for him in the dark.

Suddenly dirt and rock flew past my head. Leo tore away at the rubble, clawing furiously at it. "Gotta git out!" he wailed. "Gotta git out!"

"Leo, listen to me," I said, barely keeping the panic out of my voice. I had to stay calm for him, for both of us, if we hoped to get out of this place.

Finally, I got my arms around him and pulled him away. He fought me some, but then I heard him whimper. I held him tight. Something wet splashed against my hand. He was crying.

I pressed his hands in mine as we huddled together.

"What you doin', gal?" he sobbed.

"First things first. We need to pray."

"Pray?" he sniffed. "We need to git out's what we need to do."

"God will help us get out," I said, still trying to keep my voice steady. Somehow just saying those words made me feel braver. I hoped they would help Leo too.

"Gal, prayin' ain't gonna git us outta here," he argued. "We gotta *dig.* You hear me? *Dig!*"

I tightened my grip on his hands. "Sure, Leo, we'll dig. But first I'll ask God to watch over us."

He almost laughed. "Where was God watchin' when we got into this fix? And when Hazel crashed? And when that crazy rancher grabbed us?"

"Hush, Leo," I said. "We're in this fix because of that greedy Maddox, not God. I know God hears my prayers.

And answers them too. He promises that in the Bible."

I commenced praying. Not a long prayer. Just a few words asking for help. I didn't know if Leo prayed with me, but he hushed up at least.

We sat quietly for a while. Then I said, "We've gotta dig slow and deliberate," I said. "Or else we'll use up too much air."

Sighing heavily, he said, "I reckon you're right, gal."

"Let's just move the rock we can. One piece at a time. When we get tired, we'll rest. OK?"

He stayed silent the longest time. Finally, he answered, "I reckon."

I used a couple more matches to find out where to start. Then we set to work. Back in Oklahoma I once helped Daddy and Mama clear rocks from a field. It had been a backbreaking job. This proved much the same. The smaller rock we scooped out and tossed behind us. The larger rock we struggled with together.

"Let's jest clear out the little ones first," Leo suggested after we grappled with a big one that wouldn't budge.

"OK," I agreed, but I knew that sooner or later we'd have to move some of the big ones.

We kept after it for a long time. I couldn't tell if we made much headway, but we plumb wore ourselves out.

Finally, we stopped to rest, sitting with our backs against the cave-in. It felt cool and damp in there, but still I'd worked up a good sweat. I used my bandanna to wipe my face and arms.

"Gal," Leo said as we rested. "Sorry if I acted like a

plumb fool a while back."

I couldn't even make out the shape of him in the dark, but I heard him breathe and felt him nearby.

"Must've been that bump you took," I said.

"Nope, I was plenty scared," he admitted. "Still am. Fact is . . ."

I waited. He had something on his mind. I wouldn't rush him to tell it.

Finally, he continued, "Fact is, I've been trapped in a mine before. A coal mine. Me and some other kids were explorin' and I got lost from 'em. My pa finally found me. He whipped me good. Then just three days later my brother got killed by a wolf and Pa, well, he run off. That's the way I remember my pa. Whippin' me for gettin' lost in that mine and then runnin' off 'cause of Charley."

His story made my insides turn over. I hurt for him like he was my own true brother. I said, "I'm sorry, Leo. But what about the rest of your family?"

"Ma . . . I told you and your folks. She died when I was born."

"What about other brothers?" I asked. "Or sisters?"

He paused. "Nina is all. My big sister. She was fourteen, I think, last I seen her."

I stared into the blackness, tempted to strike a match so I could make him out. See his face, his unruly black hair, his dark eyes shining. My heart ached for this boy, so all alone and now a brother to me. "What happened to Nina?"

"Somebody took her in," he answered. "But they didn't want a boy. Not me, leastwise. So I got a ride west, out to

California." I felt him shudder next to me. "Anyway, this place reminds me of gettin' lost in that coal mine. And of Charley—and Pa. Kinda scares me. You know?"

"I know," I said. "But we'll get out of here. You'll see. I know we will." Then I reached out and put my arms around him, giving him a big hug.

"*Gal!*" he hollered, pulling away. "What in tarnation's got into you?"

Truth was, after Leo's story, I felt plain awful for being jealous of him and Hazel. My conscience nagged me plenty: *Jessie Land,* it said, *you've been selfish. Leo is your true friend and so is Hazel.* I wanted to apologize to him, but something stopped me. Maybe it was because I felt weak and scared. Maybe it was pure pride. Anyway, I kept my apology to myself.

Leo broke into my thoughts by saying, "Don't know 'bout you, gal, but I'm powerful hungry."

"Me too," I agreed. "Hungry and thirsty."

Then I remembered the California orange I'd slipped into my overalls yesterday.

I dug the orange out, bit off a piece of skin, and peeled the rest. The sweet smell of the fruit exploded in our close quarters. As I separated the sections, sticky juice ran down my hand and I licked it off. We took turns eating, a section at a time. One small piece of fruit wasn't much, but its juiciness refreshed us.

We decided to get a little shuteye before setting back to work. We huddled beside the rubble of caved-in rocks. Leo drowsed off right away. Me, I said a silent prayer: *Lord, I know You're listening. Rescue us from this fix. Please!*

I slipped into sleep. It seemed I'd just closed my eyes when Leo woke me. We went right back to work with nary a word between us.

A long time passed. My back throbbed and my arms grew weak. I slumped against the wall of rubble, feeling plumb wore out. That's when I sensed a change in the air.

"Leo, what's that?" I asked.

"What's what?"

A certain coolness drifted past my face. I struck a match and held it to the wall we'd been working on. The flame went out.

"It's *air!*" I cried out. "We broke through!" He let go a whoop that bounced around the space like a rubber ball.

Something came to me. "I got an idea," I told him.

"What?" he asked.

"If you lasso one of these big rocks, maybe we can pull down a full load at one time," I suggested.

"But what if it pulls the ceilin' down on us again?" he worried.

"We've gotta try," I said. "I don't know about you, but I can't stand it down here much longer." The one whiff of fresh air only made me ache for more.

Leo used our last matches to find the coiled rope on the ground. Then I heard him work his lasso through the opening we'd made. Soon he stood beside me again.

"Take hold," he said, putting the rope in my hands, "and pull hard."

I gripped the rope tightly and pulled. It held firm. Whatever rock he'd lassoed must've been plenty big.

We strained at the rope.

"*Pull*, gal!" he grunted. "Pull hard!"

"I *am*," I complained. "It's just not mov—"

Then it *did* move. A little. I felt a slight jolt, heard the sound of rock scraping against rock.

"*It's comin'!*" Leo shouted. "Keep pullin'!"

I put all my strength behind it. Then I felt another jolt. It *was* pulling free!

"One more time, gal!" Leo yelled.

Again we yanked hard on the rope. I felt the rock give way. The rope went slack as the rock dropped out of place.

We scrambled to the opening and felt around. Only a narrow slit, but an opening!

"Smell it, Leo!" I cried. "That sweet, sweet air!"

"I smell it, gal, and I aim to be out in it directly," Leo said, coiling up his rope and tying it to his belt.

It took little time to work the opening bigger. I told Leo to go through first. He grunted and groaned as I pushed from behind. He managed to inch his way through to the other side.

"*Made it!*" he shouted. "Come on, gal. Now you."

I was taller but thinner than Leo. For me it didn't seem too tight a squeeze.

I found my friend on the other side and hugged him. This time he didn't struggle against me. Fact was, I felt him hug me back.

"Let's get outta here!" he urged.

Keeping between the iron tracks, we felt our way along

in the darkness. After a while I began to dimly make out the walls of the mine. Then I could see the rusty rails. Then daylight!

We ran out the mine opening and shouted with joy. The bright sunlight stung our eyes, and we had to cover our faces.

Once we got used to the light, we tried to get our bearings.

"I see the sun through them trees," Leo pointed out. His dirty face and hands and clothes matched the color of his hair. "It's morning, I figure."

"Which way should we go?" I said. I looked down at my own clothes and hands. They were thoroughly covered with grime.

"I'll climb this hill and take a looksee," he said.

He raced up the mound of dirt and rock that formed the opening of the mine. I watched him steady himself on a large rock. Before long, he dashed down.

He grabbed the strap of my overalls and yanked hard. Panic flared in his eyes.

"*Gal!*" he gasped. "There's—"

"What is it?" I demanded. After all we'd been through already, I couldn't imagine what'd gotten into the boy. "Leo, for heaven's sake, what's the troub—"

His voice exploded at me. "Gal, it's the— It's the worst-lookin' *monster* I've ever seen in all my born days. And it's comin' our way!"

Chapter 15

I stared at the boy like he'd lost his wits.

"*Mon*ster?" I said. "Leo, what's gotten into you?"

His eyes didn't change, though he did let go of my overalls strap.

"Gal, I ain't joshin' you," he insisted. "There's a monster on the other side of that mound. A real 'un."

I turned away from him and looked at the mound, as if I could peer through it. Actually, though, I listened for some sound of a monster. Real or imagined. I didn't hear a thing.

Leo tugged on my arm. "We'd best head the other way, gal. He's comin' right fast."

Just then, though, I did hear something. The snap of a twig, I guessed. Then the rustle of the underbrush.

"You hear that, gal?" Leo whispered.

"I heard something," I admitted. "But land sakes, boy, it could've been a deer or a ground squirrel or a . . ."

"If it's a ground squirrel, we'd best be runnin'," he said. "I've never seen no seven-foot-tall ground squirrel with the face of a—a *demon!*"

I wanted to shake the boy. Shake him hard. There's no

accounting for the peculiar things that pop into a boy's
head. And for no apparent reason!

Instead of letting him pull me away, I slipped out of his
grasp and edged around the mound.

"Jessie!" he cried.

I kept going and he rushed up behind me. I guessed he
didn't want to be left alone, especially with a monster on
the prowl. He stood so close his breath warmed my neck.

"I don't see anything," I whispered.

"Monsters can disappear, I figure," he whispered back.

I planted my hands against the side of the mound and
peered around it. Leo clutched the back of my overalls.

Suddenly, an enormous brown snout came around the
mound and nearly pressed against my face. Two big eyes
with lashes as large as brooms stared right back at me.
The nostrils on this incredible beast flared and his head
shot back.

"Yah!" I yelled out, stumbling backward. Leo fell behind me and scrambled in the brush.

"Told you!" he shouted.

The beast stepped forward in a kind of swaying, grace-
ful manner. He had some neck on him. Long as my arm I
determined. Longer even. What on earth?

Leo hopped up and jerked the rope on his belt.

"I'll lasso the monster, gal!" he yelled. "I'll lasso 'im
and we'll escape. Jest like we did with the wolf."

I looked down at the scabbed knees of the beast and at
its wide feet. The thing started to look a little more familiar. I'd never seen one up close, but I'd seen Sunday

School pictures of them before.

"Settle down, Leo," I told my friend. "This's no monster. I take this to be a camel."

"A *what?*"

"A camel," I said. I moved around to the side of the large, lumbering creature. "See the hump. Say, look at that."

"Lookit what?"

The camel bobbed its massive head away from us and chomped at a small clump of plants growing on the mound.

"It's got a saddle," I pointed out. "And a bridle."

"What's a camel doin' in Arizona?" my friend asked, unbelieving.

"Don't know, but someone's been riding him."

I went up to the beast and patted its thick, shaggy fur. It smelled vile. I sniffed my hand. It smelled just like the camel.

"Where on earth did it come from?" I wondered aloud.

"Don't know," Leo answered, "but he's got a powerful awful smell to 'im, don't he?"

I wiped my hand on my overalls. "He does that."

The camel stopped eating long enough to gaze at us again. It batted those large, heavy eyelids and long lashes at us like it was plenty bored. Its mouth worked slowly on the clump of green.

"Lookit the awful teeth on that thing," Leo remarked. He was right. They were large and yellow and appeared in need of a good scrubbing.

I stepped carefully around the large beast, taking it in. Trying to figure out how it got here. And whether it's being here had anything to do with us being here. Leo followed on my heels, though he'd grown braver now.

"Bet he'd be a snap to rope," my friend boasted. "He's all neck." Leo had a point there.

Sunlight filtering through the trees lit up something hanging from the saddle. It glittered. I edged close to the camel and touched the shining object.

What was it?

"What're you doin' there, gal?" Leo said.

A small piece of rope tied the object to the saddle. I untied it and held the object in my hand.

"What you got there?" Leo asked.

I held my hand out so we could both see. "Remember the Spanish stirrup from that chest?"

"Yeah, that's it!" Leo cried.

"But what's it doing tied to the saddle on a camel?" I asked.

"Maybe someone found the chest," Leo suggested.

"But why tie this old stirrup to the saddle?"

Leo scratched his head.

The camel finished chewing, gave us another glance, then moseyed around the mound.

"Maybe the stirrup's a message from someone," I said.

"Someone sent a camel to find us?" Leo said, confused.

"I don't know," I confessed. "But let's follow this critter and see if any of this makes sense."

We trailed the beast, staying a little ways back.

After a bit, Leo said, "You know, gal, whoever found that stirrup musta found the chest. And maybe they found somethin' else."

"What?" I asked, though I already knew the answer. *Hazel.*

Chapter 16

I hurried along beside the camel and grabbed the reins. The creature stopped, poked its head around slowly, and eyed me good.

Coming up behind me, Leo said, "Whatcha doin', gal?"

I just stared back at the camel and jiggled the reins some. All of a sudden it bent its front legs and knelt down. Then its back legs folded up and the creature just collapsed before our eyes.

"*Wow!*" Leo exclaimed. "Didja see that? What's it doin'?"

"Sitting, Leo," I said.

"I know that," he grumbled. "I mean, why? I thought it was leadin' us somewhere."

"Maybe it is. Maybe it wants us to climb up on it."

"Whoa, gal! On *that* smelly beast? Ain't no way I'm sittin' up there on . . ."

I felt every bit as nervous as Leo, but I figured it wouldn't be saddled if it weren't fit to ride. I eased my leg up and over the saddle which perched right smack on top of the camel's hump.

"Hey, gal, watch out!" Leo cried behind me.

But I had already hoisted myself up. The camel swung

its shaggy head around and gave me another long look. Then it turned to Leo as if to say, "Well, what're *you* waiting for?"

Leo rubbed his hands on his trousers. He looked determined. "If you can do it, I can do it." Then my friend climbed up behind me.

At once the camel straightened its hind legs and jerked up its front legs.

"Whoa!" Leo and I shouted together as we bumped higher in the air.

The camel set out, taking slow steps through the forest. It walked in a funny way, plodding but steady with a kind of roll so Leo and I moved forward and up and back and down. Maybe something like being in a ship on a rocky sea. The motion didn't scare me, but I tightened my grip on the reins.

"Hey, this ain't too bad," Leo remarked. "Kick your heels a bit and let's giddyap."

"You just sit still and hush up," I told him. "I'm driving this camel."

"Yeah, but git 'im goin' faster."

"We're doing fine, considering we've never seen a camel before, much less ridden one."

As we ambled on through the forest, I wondered where we'd stop and who'd be waiting for us. Would we find Hazel? I surely hoped so. And what about the camel? I figured it must've come from the Arab lands. So how did it end up here, halfway around the world in Arizona? How strange for a camel to be traipsing through a forest littered with pine needles and not a lick of sand in sight.

Leo squirmed behind me. Then he did what I should've known he'd do. He dug his heels into the camel's sides and shouted, "Come on, camel! Git on there! Hee-yah!"

Before I could rein in, the creature reacted. It lurched forward, its long, thin legs reaching out farther and faster.

"*Leo!*" I yelled. "Why on earth did you—"

Tree limbs rushed at us. The camel ducked its large head and dodged them. But Leo and I had to bend low to keep from getting knocked to the ground.

I yanked back on the reins, but it didn't slow the beast. It rushed on through the forest in a weird kind of gait. I held tight to the saddle and the reins as we rolled and rocked along.

Leo, though, was having himself a swell time. He hollered out, "*Yahoo!* Git on there, camel! Go on, *git!*" He kicked his heels and the camel lurched. We went faster!

"*Leo!*" I shouted at him.

We took off, rocking and bumping along in what I took to be a camel gallop. I stayed low, shut my eyes tight, and clung to the creature for all the life in me.

Just when I thought sure I'd get knocked to the ground, the trees ended and the camel rushed out into open space. Straight ahead I saw the plain with the stream running through it. And beyond that the mesa with the pueblo sitting on top. After all that had happened, I half expected things to look somehow different. But nothing had changed, other than us riding the camel, of course.

The camel splashed through the stream with his big, wide feet. Still, not a drop of water touched us.

"Yee-hi!" Leo yelled in my ear. I poked him hard with my elbow. Leave it to a boy to get a thrill out of a death-defying ride on the back of a foreign critter.

The camel glided across the plain, heading straight for the base of the mesa. I feared at this speed it would smash us right into the rocky cliff. But at the last moment the creature slowed and came to a halt at the exact spot we'd climbed down yesterday.

"What a ride!" Leo exclaimed. "I'm takin' a likin' to this camel, gal."

Before I could speak, the camel dropped again. Front legs first, then the back. It happened so suddenly, Leo and I bumped off the saddle and rolled across the ground. The creature turned its massive head and stared at us, batting its eyelashes. He probably couldn't believe we'd stuck to him for the whole ride.

The camel's mouth curled back, baring its yellow teeth. It bellowed out a strange groan. I wondered if this was the sound the archeologists had heard just before they'd been spooked off. And the footprints! The beast made the same prints we'd seen yesterday.

I turned to tell Leo my discovery when I heard a shout. I couldn't make out the words, but the voice sounded strong. A raspy voice I'd know anywhere.

Hazel!

Relief flooded through me. Hazel was alive and calling to someone! But then there came another sound. A deadly sound.

"Hey!" Leo cried. "Someone's *shoot*ing up there!"

Chapter 17

Silence. Then another blast of gunfire.

I listened hard but didn't hear Hazel's voice again.

I exclaimed to Leo, "We've gotta get up there!"

"But somebody's shootin', gal," Leo said, as if I needed the reminder.

Another shot echoed in the still air.

"I'm going up," I declared, heading for the trail that led to the top of the mesa.

"Not without me you ain't," Leo replied.

We left the camel nibbling the few plants around. The mysteries of where it came from and why it had that Spanish stirrup tied to its saddle would just have to wait. I prayed as I climbed up the mesa that those shots hadn't harmed Hazel. From the sound of her voice at least, I figured she came through the plane crash OK.

As we neared the top of the mesa, the gunfire stopped. An eerie silence filled the air. What had happened? Who had fired those shots? And what about Hazel? Questions kept flashing through my mind. Questions with no answers.

Leo pulled up behind me.

"Gal, what you figure's goin' on?"

"I wish I knew," I said as I peered over the top of the cliff.

The campsite, the pueblo—everything looked just like we'd left it yesterday. I caught a movement by the pueblo and squinted in that direction. I spied a flash of gray near the ground. What was it? I looked harder and saw a person lying there. The movement I'd noticed proved to be the person's shirt rustling in the breeze. Who—

At that second I recognized her. *"Hazel!"*

I sprang up and scrambled toward her. I heard Leo racing behind me.

Hazel looked up. She wore white bandages wrapped around her head, her left hand, and her right foot. A tree limb stripped of bark leaned against the wall beside her. When she spotted us running toward her, she waved her arm.

"Git down!" she shouted. "Git down!"

I ignored her, not stopping until I threw my arms around her. I hugged her hard.

"O, Hazel," I cried, "are you OK?"

She squeezed me, then reached over to hug Leo. Did I imagine that she clung to him longer than she had to me?

"I'm sorta OK," she said. "Fact is, the strangest thing happened. It was like the trees helped break the ol' Waco's fall. Oh, it tore my plane good, ripped the wings off and all. But as the fuselage crashed toward the ground, the limbs kept slowin' me down, almost like arms grabbin' and cradlin' me. It was plumb strange. I just got a few bumps. Though busted my ankle I 'spect." She eyed

me and Leo good. "I'll swear you two look like you've
been mining coal."

I glanced at my dusty overalls and Leo's blackened
face.

"We got trapped in a mine," I told her. "Cal Maddox—"

"*Maddox!* That scoundrel!"

Before I could explain all that had happened, another
gunshot rang out. A chunk of adobe exploded above our
heads.

"Who's the varmint doin' the shootin'?" Leo asked.

"I'll give you three guesses," Hazel replied.

But we didn't need any guesses. Maddox's voice thundered from across the plaza.

"Turn over that chest, Hazel," he yelled, "and I'll let
those upstarts go. I'll let you all go peacefully."

Just hearing his voice riled me. "Upstarts! He's talking
about us!"

"Sure as shootin'," Hazel replied. "He yelled out earlier that he had you and Leo tied up somewhere. That he
wouldn't let you loose till I gave him the chest."

"He's plumb crazy," Leo said.

Maddox fired more shots and chunks of adobe rained
down on us again.

I crouched beside Hazel and said, "There's no sense
getting ourselves killed over a bunch of old relics. Let's
just give him the chest. Then he'll leave us alone."

"I ain't so sure he'd really leave us alone," Hazel said.

I tried to spot Maddox's hiding place. I couldn't see
him. He didn't even have the courage to face us directly.

Only a coward hid and used guns to bully folks.

"Hazel, just give him the chest," I pleaded, tired of lying in the dirt and spitting dust. Tired of going up against the likes of Cal Maddox.

"I would, but ..." she began.

"But what?"

"I don't reckon Robert'll let me."

I gazed at her, not understanding. *Who?*

Hazel didn't answer. Instead, she sat up and glanced around.

I looked across the plaza of the old pueblo. The wind picked up dust and weeds and threw them into the air. No sound came from the deserted ruin.

Peeking over the adobe wall, Hazel said, "Maddox is up to something. He's probably doubling back so he can come up behind us."

She grabbed the stripped tree limb beside her and struggled to her feet. Leo and I helped her as best we could.

"Who's this Robert?" I asked. I didn't want to add another mystery to the list I'd been storing in my head. Like the phantom and the flute playing. And Areana and her so-called brother. And the camel. And—

But my questioning stopped when I caught sight of something odd in a doorway. It looked like a piece of black cloth blowing in the wind.

What was that?

I stared at the wall. The black cloth fluttered again against the tan-colored adobe. A shirt! And wearing it a man. He'd just crawled through the opening.

At first I ducked down, thinking only of that vile snake Cal Maddox. But Hazel saw him too, and she made no effort to flee. In fact, she raised her arm and waved.

And the stranger, dressed all in black, waved back, signaling us to come.

Chapter 18

Hazel hobbled toward the dark figure, using the tree limb as a crutch. "Come on," she called back to us.

"Wait," I said. "Who is that?"

"We can't stay here. Maddox'll find us."

Leo and I looked at each other, confused. How did this mysterious person fit in with all the other strange goings on? But Hazel was right about Cal Maddox. We needed to hide—and in a hurry.

Dust puffed up from the ground as we trotted after Hazel.

We caught up with her as she reached the stranger. Then I noticed the wall behind him.

The fresh adobe! This was the very spot we'd broken through to discover the chest. The same spot we'd found repatched later. Now a new rectangular opening had been cut in the wall. The day-old adobe lay heaped beside the opening. Would the chest be inside?

I looked at the strange man. He had a kind of black shawl draped over his shoulders and head, forming a hood. I could only make out a bit of his dark, unshaven face. He wore black pants and a faded, black shirt with frayed cuffs. His black, denim jacket had small brass buttons. On his feet he wore dusty, buckskin moccasins.

He stood gazing away, as if watching for signs of Maddox. Hazel didn't speak. It seemed like they had some kind of secret language between them because when he stepped aside she ducked down and hobbled through the low doorway.

Leo and I looked at each other.

"Gal, I don't like this," he whispered.

Before I could answer, the man reached out and grasped my arm. His fingers felt cool. He gently steered me toward the opening. I didn't know what to make of him, but I trusted Hazel. I crawled inside. Leo followed close behind me. Probably he didn't want to be left alone with the likes of this stranger.

Inside the room, a small oil lamp burned in one corner. The flickering light revealed the cracked and bowed adobe walls. I eyed the ceiling. Through the broken mud I saw chunks of wood and mud and patches of sunlight. What had Hazel warned? A good sneeze might bring it down?

Hazel sat in a corner and adjusted her bandages. She propped her injured foot on something. The chest!

I hurried over to her.

"What's this all about?" I asked her.

"All in good time, child," she replied.

I have to admit her mysterious manner began to irritate me. I'm something of a plain-facts girl. I like sensible answers to sensible questions. I don't have much regard for secrets and spooky-acting folks.

Then the stranger came through the opening. He went to the middle of the room and stood looking at the chest. Something about the way he moved and his muscular build told me he was a young man.

He unwrapped the shawl and tossed it into the corner. I gasped at the sight of him.

Though he needed a shave and haircut, I recognized his face at once. He was none other than the young man in Areana's painting. The same delicate eyebrows. The same large, dark, angry eyes, eyes that shone like black gems. The same hard mouth.

"Introduce me to your friends, Hazel," he said in a soft, melodic voice that didn't go with his mouth or his eyes. "Though this one seems to know me." He nodded at me.

"Why sure 'nough," Hazel barked. "Jessie Land, Leo Little Wolf, meet Robert Rodriquez."

Rodriquez? I figured it would be Maddox. Well, maybe that was just the name he was using.

He stepped over and held out a hand to Leo. My friend took the stranger's hand and shook it. When it came my turn, I held back.

"I won't bite," he said without smiling.

"I'm not so sure of that," I declared. "If you're Areana Maddox's brother, Cal Maddox's son, you're very likely to bite."

A puzzled look crossed his face. Then his face changed and he nodded to himself. "Areana said you saw my portrait. And that she told you I was her brother. But she was just protecting me. I'm not a Maddox, I assure you."

Now I was really confused. "Well, then, maybe you can explain all the crazy things that've been going on around here," I said. "Crazy things like—"

Robert Rodriquez put his finger to his lips to shush me. He turned toward the doorway and crouched down. He seemed to be listening for something outside. I fidgeted. My patience with him, with Hazel, with this whole trip had been used up.

He stood again and faced me. "I'll explain in due time. I'm sure you have many questions."

"And I got a couple of my own," Leo spouted. "Like whose camel brought us here? And what's a critter like that doin' in Arizona anyway?"

"Once, many camels lived in Arizona," Robert answered. "They were brought in before the Civil War to carry loads. Later, folks just let the poor creatures loose to wander the state. You'd see one of them standing atop an Arizona sand dune and think you'd lost your mind. But Mirabelle, she is a fine beast. A little stubborn, but well trained. I got her from a circus."

"*Mirabelle?*" Leo said.

"Good name for a camel, don't you think?"

Normally this talk would interest me, but at that moment I wanted answers, *real* answers. "Are you the phantom?" I blurted out.

Robert Rodriquez gazed at me with that same hostile expression I'd seen in the portrait. He didn't smile and his eyes looked angry.

Shaking his head slightly, he said, "My father is Spanish and my mother Hopi. I've done nothing but try to protect the old things. I can't account for the names people stick on me."

I didn't know if he had answered my question or not. I guessed he had, that he'd just owned up to being the phantom. Though he didn't call himself by that name.

"Have I seen you before?" I asked. "Like two nights ago, in the shadows?"

Robert didn't speak. Instead, he pulled a thin, stick-looking object from his jacket pocket. He put it to his mouth and blew out a soft melody. The flute!

Returning it to his pocket, he said, "I admit I was trying to scare all of you away."

"Scare us away?" I said. "But this is Hazel's land."

"No, not Hazel's land," he said firmly, his eyes blazing. "Once it belonged to all people. And this village, this pueblo, it belonged to *my* people. Now strangers rake through the old pueblos and take everything away. Soon there'll be nothing left of my ancestors' cities but dry husks of buildings, like the dry husks of locusts."

I felt like he had somehow attacked Hazel with his words. Anger flared up in me. "Well, you got the chest back again. You took what you wanted, didn't you?"

"Jessie—" Hazel began.

I ignored her and went on. "Maybe you did something to the plane too. To make it crash. Just because this land belonged to your ancestors doesn't give you the right to go around hurting folks."

"Child, he *helped* me after the plane crashed," Hazel pointed out. "Patched me up good and decent."

"Still, he came back to steal the chest!" I accused.

"No, I *want* Hazel to take the chest," Robert insisted. "I repatched this adobe and brought the chest back inside here to keep it out of Maddox's reach."

"What?"

"I want Hazel to take it to the museum," Robert went on. "Spanish treasures belong in a museum, not in the pueblo. And I did nothing to Hazel's plane."

Leo broke in, "But what about those folks digging on the reservation? You spooked them and sent them packing."

Robert sighed. "Yes, the so-called archeologists. They were digging on Hopi land. They worked for Maddox."

"Well, I heard tell you—or the phantom anyway—used to work for Maddox," Hazel said. "That you even found this chest for him in the first place."

Just then I heard a voice outside. A familiar voice.

"Areana," I said.

Robert spun around and rushed to the opening. He dropped to his knees and peered out. I thought I heard him repeat her name under his breath. He stayed there a long time as if waiting to catch a glimpse of her. Finally, he got up and faced us.

"It's true," he said. "I worked for Maddox at one time. He knew of the Spanish chest and hired me to search for it. I thought if I found it and gave it to him ... well, that ..."

"That what?" I asked.

His eyes shot to me. "That I might win Areana's hand." He laughed unexpectedly, harshly. "I was a fool."

"You ain't a fool to love someone," Hazel told him.

His mouth grew harder, his eyes bitter. "I was a fool to believe I could have Areana. You don't name a child Areana and then give her away to some poor half-breed."

"What's her name mean?" Leo asked.

I knew not a word of Spanish, but I knew the answer to that question. I told my almost-brother, "It means silver."

"So that map—the one on the skin—really is to a treasure?" Leo asked.

Hazel explained, "The chest may've belonged to an expedition of Spaniards back in the 1500s. Maddox probably thinks they discovered a cache of silver and mapped the location. Then when they came back later for it, they got lost or Indians made off with the chest containing the map."

"Why didn't you tell us all this when we first found the chest?" I asked Hazel.

"I've just put the pieces together," she said, "after Robert here told me some things." She took her injured foot off the chest and rubbed it with her good hand.

I glanced around at the four of us, hiding inside a mud room with a rotten old chest, all because of some vile, silver-crazed man with a gun. It didn't make a lick of sense. Not one lick. I thought quickly. I had to do something to put a stop to this foolishness. It took only a moment to decide.

Bending down, I grabbed one of the handles of the chest and started pulling it across the dirt floor. "I'm giving this to Maddox," I declared.

"Jessie Land, what's got into you?" Hazel said.

"We can't keep hiding out. If we give him what he wants, he'll surely let us go." I pulled harder.

Then Robert shot over and planted his foot on the chest. "He'll not get it. It doesn't belong to him."

"It doesn't belong to you either," I argued.

"No, but it belongs to my Spanish ancestors. And Maddox can't have it."

I gripped the handle tighter and tried to pull it out from under his foot. It didn't budge.

I looked him in the eye and declared, "I think you might be as bull-headed as Cal Maddox himself." His hard look told me he didn't like my words.

"I don't care if Maddox charges in here with his guns blazing," Robert announced. "He'll not get this chest. *Never!*"

Chapter 19

Hazel piped up. "Robert, whatever happens to that durn chest don't concern me now. I've gotta get these kids to safety. There's a madman out there and sooner or later he'll come stormin' in here."

Determination burned in Robert's eyes. "I think you'd better stay put."

"Well, that's the difference 'tween me and you," she declared. "I'm thinkin' 'bout more than myself." Then, with Leo and me helping, she painfully got to her feet.

Robert started to speak, but Hazel snatched up her crutch and scooted us toward the door. "Come on, cowboys and cowgirls, let's git outta here."

We went from the dimly lit pueblo room out into the harsh, sunlit day. I squinted and shielded my eyes.

"Head back to the campsite," Hazel whispered. "And keep your voices down. Don't want to attract Maddox."

Blinking to get used to the light, I led the way around the edge of the plaza. Rock and debris crunched under our shoes.

We passed the tall heap of rubble I'd chased the phantom around two nights ago. A good place to hide, even in daylight.

Just then I heard a noise behind us. I stopped dead still. Leo ran smack into me.

"Gal!" he complained. "What—"

I spun around and clamped my hand over his mouth. I'd heard a click. The click of a gun being cocked.

"All right, don't make a move."

His awful voice made me want to yell for help. But yelling wouldn't do any good now.

"Turn yourselves around," Maddox ordered.

We turned and faced the villain.

The silver on his clothes and hands reflected the sun's light and glittered in my eyes. Sunlight reflected off the barrel of his rifle. He must've come from behind the rubble pile. He'd been hiding there just waiting for us.

"I'm takin' these children out," Hazel declared.

The rancher turned his attention to Leo and me.

"Those upstarts are something else," he said with a sneer. "They can protect themselves."

*"Every*one needs protection from you," I sassed. "You brought on all this trouble."

"Hush!" he spat.

His harsh words and the rifle silenced me.

"Now the truth," he said, turning to Hazel. "Where's the chest?"

How I wished I'd never had the misfortune of meeting this scoundrel! If only we could get fully free and clear of him. But that cocked rifle didn't offer much hope.

"Don't know what chest you're talkin' about," Hazel

said. "But we're goin'. Leave us be, you hear me?"

"You don't realize what a person like me'll do when someone stands in my way," he said, putting a bite into each word. "I want what's rightfully mine."

I confess that got to me. "That chest is no more yours than the stars in heaven. It was found on Indian land."

"Found by my hired men."

"Still, you've no right to—"

"I'll not listen to the opinions of a small fry such as yourself," he interrupted. "Now. The chest."

When we didn't answer, Maddox glanced back at the doorway we'd come through.

"I'll bet it's in there," he remarked. He turned and stared right at the very opening we'd come through.

I swallowed hard. I didn't care a whit for the chest, but I didn't want him to find Robert, didn't want harm to come to anyone. Maddox's words ran through my head: *you don't realize what a person like me'll do when someone stands in my way.*

"Wait!" I cried as he took a step toward the doorway. He eyed me suspiciously.

"I'll take you to the chest," I said quickly.

"Jessie, don't!" Hazel snapped.

I looked at her. Surely she didn't think I was about to lead Maddox to where Robert was hiding. Though, fact was, I had no plan, not even an idea of what to do.

Maddox threatened, "Get going, upstart!"

My eyes went to the pueblo house we'd just come from. A rickety ladder leaned against the wall near the opening. It gave me an idea.

I pointed to the roof. "Up there. See for yourself."

Maddox smiled grimly. "You lead the way."

"Leave her be, Maddox," Hazel warned, but her words were no match for that rifle of his.

You are plumb crazy, Jessie Land, I told myself as I headed for the ladder with Maddox trailing close. Fear knocked in my heart, but I prayed with every step that this awful situation would come to a peaceful end. And soon!

Chapter 20

I hadn't quite reached the ladder when Leo rushed up beside me. His eyes set firm, he popped a stick of chewing gum into his mouth.

"I'm comin' along, gal," he announced.

I smiled, glad to have him with me but worried about what lay ahead.

Hazel yelled at Maddox, "Return those youngsters back to me at once!" Maddox paid her no mind and Hazel couldn't chase after him what with her foot banged up and all.

Then I heard other footsteps rush up behind us. I looked back and spied Areana in a bright-blue dress.

"Please, Father!" she cried. "Stop!"

Maddox spun around and ordered, "Get back to the car."

Areana shook her long black hair. It caught on the breeze like a plume of smoke, then dropped back to her shoulders. Her dark eyes brimmed with tears. She reached for her father, but he stepped back.

"Why must you do this?" she pleaded. "Leave these children alone."

"Not till I get the map!" he argued. "It leads to more silver than you can even imagine."

"Silver! Is that all you live for?"

"Areana, I told you to go back to the car," Maddox said. "Don't disobey me."

"I'm *not* going back," his daughter replied, her lips trembling. I could tell that she feared him. That it took everything in her to stand up to the man.

He shrugged and turned from her. "Suit yourself, but that doesn't change anything," he said. Then, pointing his rifle at Leo and me, he growled, "Up the ladder."

I went first. My hands grasped the rough wood of the ladder's sides. With the first two rungs broken, I stepped high to get a foot on the third rung. I eased my weight on it. It held. I went up, step by step, careful to test each rung to see if it would hold me.

Leo came next. Maddox followed us before Leo even reached the top. The ladder creaked under his weight. I hoped the rotten wood would give way, spilling Maddox to the ground. Then maybe we could make a run for it. But the ladder held.

At the top I stood on the edge of the roof. It looked like a wall—just laid out flat. Here and there where the adobe had worn away I saw crisscrossed poles and a few thicker logs underneath.

It struck me at that moment that this was the same roof I nearly fell from the night Areana rescued me. I spied the crumbled corner where the roof had given way. And at this very moment Robert and the chest were just beneath us! Maybe coming up here had been a mistake. I must be careful!

As Maddox stepped onto the roof and stood beside us, I saw Areana making her way up the ladder too.

"OK, upstarts, where's that chest?" Maddox demanded.

Think, Jessie! I told myself.

Leo and I gazed over the roofs of the pueblo. Those that hadn't caved in stretched out before us like a patchwork of box tops. I noticed another adobe house stacked on top of the level we stood on. Leo noticed it too. He pointed to its roof.

"It's up there, ain't it, gal?" he said, winking at me.

At once, I nodded and said, "Yes, that's where it is."

Maddox looked hard at the both of us, then at the rooftop, then back at us. "It better be," he warned.

If only I had some kind of plan. It wouldn't take Maddox long to realize this was just another wild-goose chase.

Rifle slung over one shoulder, Maddox pulled up the ladder and dragged it to the wall of the next house. All the while I kept trying to come up with a real plan. I at least needed to get Robert out from under this dangerous roof. I glanced at Areana, but her eyes looked empty and she seemed lost in her own world.

Just then Leo nudged me and whispered, "Gal, how 'bout I rope that villain and we hogtie him good?"

"No, Leo," I whispered back, "if he falls on this roof it's liable to cave in. And Robert's under us."

Maddox propped the ladder against the nearby wall. He started to climb. I waited till he got halfway up, then I leaned over the edge of the roof and screamed, *"Robert, get out! Run!"*

The rancher glared at me from his perch on the ladder. Muttering, he scampered down.

I raced along the edge of the roof, shouting *"Get out, Robert! Hazel, tell him to get out!"*

Below, I heard feet crunching on the dry ground. Peering down, I spotted Robert and Hazel in the plaza. They looked up and saw me.

"Jessie, Leo, stay on the edge!" Hazel called. "It's not safe!"

I waved and yelled, *"Go on, get away!* We're coming!"

I turned just as Maddox snatched Leo.

"Lemme go, you outlaw!" my friend shouted.

Clutching Leo, Cal Maddox roared at me, "You've been in it from the start with that blamed Rodriquez. Well, you'd best tell me now where that chest really is or your friend's future don't look too good."

"Areana, stop him," I called, not really knowing what she could do.

I glanced at her. She stood frozen on the far side of the roof, her eyes darting between me and her father.

"I'll make you two upstarts sorry you ever crossed me," Maddox snarled.

Leo struggled, his arms and legs flying about, but he was powerless against the rancher's strength.

The truth hit me hard: Leo had no one to count on but me. I needed to free him from this madman's grasp, and fast.

I ran to Maddox and tried to wrench his arm from Leo, but the villain had my friend bundled up tighter than a bale of hay. Maddox reached out and grabbed hold of my overalls. He had us both!

"Got you!" he said, his mouth in a twisted grin.

I kicked at him, tried to punch him with my fists. But he held me out so my blows cut through air. I could feel the strength of his grip. He still had one arm tight around Leo, pinning the boy's arms to his sides.

"Father, stop!" Areana cried.

He ignored her, wrestling me closer.

"Do you take me for a joshin' man?" he growled.

"Lemme go, you brute!" I yelled. I struck his chest with my fist, but my arms felt like jelly against his might.

"You heard the gal, Maddox!" Leo shouted. "Let us go!"

Below, I heard Hazel and Robert shouting. Then I heard the rustle of Areana's skirt and her footsteps.

"Father, let them *go!"* Areana screamed.

She came running across the roof, her arms outstretched as if she would embrace us.

"Stay clear, Areana," Maddox ordered, shaking Leo and me. We swung in the air like rag dolls. "This has nothing to do with you."

"Let us go!" I shouted. Then, for an instant, his arm appeared right in front of my face. I saw my chance and bit down hard.

He yelled and dropped us both. I grabbed Leo and we scrambled away.

"Thunderation!" he howled.

Areana stood in the middle of the roof now, watching the scene with wide, disbelieving eyes. Maddox paid her no mind and started after us again. My eyes fixed on the ladder, so far away. We had only a second—but we had to try to reach it.

"Leo!" I cried. "The ladder!"

We shot across the roof, right past Areana.

Maddox rushed after us. With each of his heavy strides, I felt the roof quake. In my mind I saw Maddox's silver-toed boots stomping the ancient adobe.

Finally, we reached the ladder. Maddox roared behind us, *"Come back here!"* But we scrambled up.

Then I heard Areana's cry. Gripping the ladder, I swung my head around and looked at the two of them.

Areana had thrown herself in Maddox's way, her hands tight around her father's arm. He lost his balance and stumbled. Both of them crashed to the roof. I saw the roof crack and begin to pull apart.

Areana hopped to her feet and started in my direction. Her father shouted, *"Areana!"*

But the warning came too late. She took one step and the whole roof gave way, pitching Areana and her father headlong into the ruin below.

Chapter 21

The pounding of my heart echoed the thundering collapse of the roof. My whole body shaking, I climbed down off the ladder. Leo and I edged near the gaping hole in the roof. I stared into the rising dust trying to see where Areana and her father had fallen. I listened but no sound came from down there.

"We've got to get to them," I told Leo.

"Already workin' on it, gal," Leo replied.

He lassoed the top of the heavy wooden ladder, pulled tight, and dropped the end of the rope down the hole in the roof. We slid down the rope into the dust-filled adobe room.

Coughing, I flapped my arms, hoping to clear the air some. I held my bandanna over my mouth and nose and started to search.

Before we could find Areana and her father, Hazel hobbled into the collapsed house. She grabbed me and hugged me good. I stood back as she hugged Leo too.

"Thank goodness you're OK!" she cried. "When I heard the roof give way, I feared you'd been hurt."

"Hazel, we've gotta help—" I began.

Robert suddenly rushed past us. *"Areana!"* he called
out as he searched for his beloved.

We could make out a patch of bright-blue cloth. Then a
pair of legs. Areana!

"Oh, the dear child!" Hazel gasped.

At that same moment I heard Maddox's voice. "Areana,
Areana," he whimpered. His voice had lost its fury. He
sounded like a broken man. As broken as the roof.

I stepped through the rubble toward him. As I waved
the dust away, I saw Maddox kneeling beside his daughter. He held her limp arm and sobbed her name. Areana
lay still, her eyes closed. Through the cloud of dust I
smelled her sweet fragrance. A few feet from the rancher,
the Spanish chest he'd hungered for sat forgotten in the
dust.

Robert swept down on the other side of Areana and
wiped the dirt from her face with his shawl. Then he
bundled the shawl, placing it under her head for a pillow.
His face grim, he put his head to her chest, listening for
signs of life. As he listened, his mouth formed a faint
smile.

"She's alive," he said quietly.

Maddox gasped. "Alive? I thought I'd lost her like—"

Hazel hobbled up behind us. "We'd best get her out
quickly. But be careful."

"We need something we can use for a stretcher," Robert said.

"I've got some wooden slats and a bedroll back at the
campsite," Hazel offered.

Robert hurried out.

Areana's eyes blinked open. She looked surprised and confused. Spotting Maddox, she said, weakly, "Father?"

He clutched her hand and gasped, "I'm here."

"What hap—"

"The roof caved in," I told her. "You fell."

She shut her eyes for a moment, then she looked at her father again.

"Father," Areana began weakly.

"Yes, Areana, what is it?" Maddox replied. It seemed strange to hear the man speak words of tenderness after all the vile things he'd said earlier.

"Can you see what . . . your passion for . . . silver has brought?" Areana spoke with a broken voice. Every breath seemed to hurt her. "This."

He dropped his eyes and looked away.

"This is what . . . what became of Mother," Areana whispered. "Your dream . . . her nightmare. You must stop. Must stop."

Maddox looked at Hazel and Leo and me with sorrowful eyes. "Maybe I've been wrong," he confessed.

"You stuck us in that mine," Leo burst in. "We could've been kilt dead from that cave-in."

The rancher choked out the words, "I'm sorry for that, boy. Areana—she spoke the truth. My wife . . . she . . . I don't know." He shook his head sadly. "Maybe she'd still be alive if I hadn't been such a fool for silver."

It seemed I'd spent my whole time in Arizona trying to escape this man. Now I almost felt pity for him.

For a moment we all stood silent. Adobe dust settled around us. It felt like peace had finally come to this old pueblo.

Leo poked me and whispered, "Gal, maybe you oughta tell 'im 'bout prayin'."

Chapter 22

As it turned out, Areana had broken both legs and two ribs. Cal Maddox had broken his arm, though I never knew it till later. He made nary a complaint about the pain.

But it was Robert who took charge of rescuing Areana. Her gaze fixed on him as he helped carry her out of the pueblo. I saw her eyes go soft and funny-looking, mirroring his own. I took it as a sign of the love between them.

All six of us rode to the Flagstaff hospital in Maddox's noisy automobile. The doctor set Hazel's broken ankle. Her other injuries were mere scrapes and bruises. Quite a wonder considering her crash in the forest!

Hazel then took Leo and me to her house and laid out enough food for ten hungry kids.

That evening two exciting things happened.

The first being that Hazel's brother Henry came home.

Folks seeing him wouldn't likely take Henry to be Hazel's brother since he was bald and scrawny and soft-spoken and all. Anyway, he looked plenty surprised to see us. Hazel told him some of what happened and his eyes grew plenty big. Then he made quite a to-do about Ha-

zel's ankle, but she pushed him away and would have no
fretting about it.

"Whoever was interested in those houses of ours
must've changed his mind," Henry remarked. "I waited
all day for someone to show up, but no one ever did."

"That's 'cause it was all a hoax," Hazel declared. "Cal
Maddox admitted himself he had some fella call. Thought
we'd both go to Phoenix to sell the property. He just
wanted us out of the way."

"Whatever for?" asked Henry.

"He guessed Robert Rodriquez to be the phantom," his
sister replied. "And he suspected Robert hid the chest at
the pueblo. Maybe he figured if he could get us away from
there, he'd have a good chance of finding the chest and
the map to the silver fortune. Course, I took a gander at
that so-called map. Not enough markings left on it to lead
you anywhere 'cept nowhere."

"Hazel, was it Maddox who caused your plane to
crash?" I asked.

"Naw," she replied, waving her hand. "I should've
checked that durn fuel line before I took off."

Henry's eyes darted to me. "Oh gosh, I almost forgot.
Jessie, I got someone who wants to see you."

He dashed out the front door. I glanced at Hazel and
she just shrugged, but the smile on her face told me she
knew something.

When he came back inside, Henry carried an apple
crate. I realized at once what he held.

"Victoria!" I cried.

I ran to him and made him put down the crate. Dipping my hands into the straw, I fetched out the baby armadillo I'd found alongside a New Mexico highway weeks earlier. Victoria rolled into a ball, and I noticed she'd grown much larger. Henry had cared for her in a right proper way.

Leo gave Victoria the once over.

"Gal, that's the strangest-lookin' critter I ever did lay eyes on," he declared. "Next to a camel, of course."

"I think you'd better take Victoria back to California when you go," Henry told me. "She's missed you."

Just then the second exciting thing happened.

A loud knock came at the front door. Hazel went to answer it and returned with an envelope in her hand.

"A telegram, Jessie," she said. "For you."

My eyes widened. A telegram! I'd never received such a thing in my life. I handed Victoria to Leo and took the envelope. I held it for the longest time, just turning it over in my hands.

"It's customary to open those things so you can read the message," Hazel remarked with a coarse laugh.

I ran my finger under the flap and opened the envelope. I pulled out the thin, yellow paper and unfolded it.

"Well, gal, don't keep us guessin'," Leo cried.

Glancing at the funny-looking message, I read out loud:

"JESSIE
    HOPE YOU ARE HAVING EXCITING TIME
STOP GOOD NEWS STOP YOUR FRIEND TOM IS
IN ARIZONA SHOOTING A MOVING PICTURE

STOP SAYS HE WILL CONTACT YOU STOP WE
MISS YOU TERRIBLY
    LOVE MAMA"

"Tom!" I exclaimed. Suddenly, I felt very happy, happi-
er even than seeing Victoria again. To Leo I said, "Tom's
coming! Remember? I told you all about him. How he
helped me get to California."

Ignoring my excitement, Leo asked, "What's all that
STOP business?" He wore a frown on his face and gave
Victoria back to me.

"Telegram writing," Henry explained. "They use
STOP instead of a period."

Everyone seemed pleased except Leo. After a while, I
saw him slip out of the room. I didn't know what to make
of that boy. I went looking for him and found him in the
backyard twirling his lasso.

He didn't even look up when the screen door slammed
behind me.

"Want to hold Victoria?" I asked, but he didn't answer.

"Now, don't go being rude to my pet," I advised him.

"I don't care much for associatin' with armadillos," he
said, dropping the lasso to the ground.

"What's wrong?" I asked.

"Nothin'."

"Leo Little Wolf, don't lie to me. Your face is as long as
an Oklahoma dirt road. Quit pouting like a spoiled child
and talk to me."

He gave me a sidelong glance. "Must be pretty nice

gettin' a telegram like that," he muttered. "I never had so much as a letter from no one. And havin' all these friends you got."

So that was it. Feeling sorry for himself.

"Leo, I'm learning fast what having a brother means," I told him. "Sometimes it's trouble, pure and simple."

"Well, I've noticed you don't seem too pleased havin' me about lately," he pouted.

Right then I felt low as a garden snake. Lower even.

"Leo, I—" I began.

"You don't have to say nothin'."

"Hush up, boy, and let me say it." At first I kept my eyes down, on Victoria. Then I looked up, swallowed hard, and confessed, "I don't know what got into me. I guess I felt . . . jealous."

"Jealous of *me?*" he asked, surprised.

I nodded. "Of you and Hazel. The way she took to you and all. That jealousy haunted me like . . . like a phantom. I know now I was wrong. God doesn't want us to be jealous. I'm sorry, Leo. I just hope you'll forgive me."

My almost-brother popped a stick of gum in his mouth and chomped on it. He seemed to be thinking things over. The worry drained from his face as he pulled in his rope, coiled it, and tied it to his belt.

"I reckon you didn't mean no harm," he said. "Besides, I reckon you're stuck with me, like it or not." He reached out and lifted Victoria from my arms. "Lemme see this here critter."

"Be gentle," I instructed.

He looked from the armadillo to me.

"What are you doin'?" I asked.

"Just noticin' somethin'."

"Noticin' what?"

"Noticin' how much she looks like you," he chuckled.

My eyebrows shot up.

"I'll get you, boy!" I exclaimed.

I chased him all around the yard, and we ran laughing under the dark Flagstaff sky. When I caught up with him, I planned to give that boy a big hug, like it or not. And I figured he'd let go of one whale of a shriek.

Just like a brother.

ABOUT THE AUTHOR

Jerry Jerman lives in Norman, Oklahoma with his wife Charlene, twin daughters Emily and Hadley, son Andrew, and two cats. He likes Mexican food, baseball, traveling throughout the American Southwest, and really fast roller coasters. When he's not writing about the journeys of Jessie Land, he keeps busy with church and family activities. Now and then he does something crazy like late October sailboat racing in a "frostbite regatta."

More Journeys of Jessie Land!

#1 The Long Way Home

When 12-year-old Jessie Land finds herself "dumped" on uncaring relatives, she determines to run away and find her parents in California. That means a desperate journey across the south-central U.S. during the Dust Bowl of 1935.

How will Jessie get from Liberal, Kansas to San Bernardino, California in only one week? That's all the time she has before her parents move on in their search for work.

Follow Jessie's exciting adventures as she joins two travelers, and stands up to danger and fear — armed with her faith, a tattered Bible, and her love for an orphaned armadillo named Victoria.

More Journeys of Jessie Land!

#2 My Father the Horse Thief

*J*essie Land — happily reunited with her parents in California — soon finds herself in the middle of trouble.

Her father's new job on Will Rogers' Santa Monica ranch opens the door to disaster when Rogers' favorite horse, Soapsuds, turns up missing. Worse yet — Jessie's father also has disappeared. Soon after that, a ransom note for Soapsuds appears — in *his* handwriting.

With the help of her new friend, Leo Little Wolf, Jessie bravely searches for her father, encountering a dangerous wolf and even more dangerous men who want her father to be found guilty of the crime.

Join Jessie as she finds herself on a journey testing both her faith in God and in her father's innocence.

More Journeys of Jessie Land!

#4 Danger at Outlaw Creek

Wherever she travels, twelve-year-old Jessie Land finds herself caught up in action and adventure.

In her latest journey — this time to Southern Arizona — Jessie teams up with her old friend Tennessee Tom, who needs her help on the movie set of a western called *Danger at Outlaw Creek*.

Jessie quickly finds herself tangling with ruthless Iola Linville, a corrupt woman who plots against Tom and who will stop at nothing to get what she wants.

Jessie's troubles pile up as she bravely faces each new danger. In the midst of the struggle to outwit Iola, Jessie is reminded of God's generosity to those who learn to trust Him.